ONE HUNDRED APACHES IN FULL WAR PAINT

suddenly emerged from the night, ringing the frightened women and sending chills down the spines of the helpless men. They closed in, silent, ominous, rifles in their hands.

"What do they want?" someone asked Cort.

"They want Pearson," he said tonelessly.

"Damn you, Cort!" Pearson screamed and his hand flashed to his hip. The darkness was split by the roar of six-shooters.

Cort turned and stumbled. A woman's scream cut the night as he fell back into the arms of Red Calf. . . .

TOMBSTONE STAGE

William Hopson

MB

A MACFADDEN-BARTELL BOOK

THIS IS THE COMPLETE TEXT
OF THE ORIGINAL EDITION

A MACFADDEN BOOK..................1970

Macfadden-Bartell Corporation
A subsidiary of Bartell Media Corporation
205 East 42nd Street, New York, New York 10017

Chapter One

JIM CORT awoke in his camp that night, aware that something was very much wrong. He didn't know why; perhaps because he was getting a little nervous and uneasy of late. This thing had begun to get on his nerves during the past few weeks. It had been that way, he thought, ever since he had decided he'd had enough of smuggling and was going to quit.

He came up on an elbow, the .44 pistol he always kept beneath his pillow gripped in his right hand. He lay in his blankets under the cottonwoods, listening. The campfire long since had died down to a bed of ash-covered coals. The trees were silent except for the occasional sleepy twitter of a bird. Overhead, a Mexican moon, crescent-shaped, looked down upon the shallow waters of the *Rio de la Concepcion*. For this was south of the Arizona Territory-Sonora border line; the camp was his headquarters.

A glance at the blankets of his Apache helper, Red Calf, showed them to be empty. The Indian was gone, faded like the shadows around the camp.

Cort came up noiselessly and slipped on a pair of moccasins: handiwork of a wild woman of the murderous Sonora Apaches who were too often slipping across the Arizona Territory to join their northern brethren in deadly raids.

He wasn't too worried about Red Calf insofar as loyalty

was concerned. The pay was too good, and so was the whiskey Cort usually brought back from Tucson for Red Calf and the members of his family. It was Jim Cort's ticket of safety among the meanest, most vicious branch of the Indian tribes known to white men. That and the fact that he had saved the Indian's life. They were as a whole, cruel and murderous, and too many American cavalry officers up north of the line were finding out to their sorrow how slippery the dark-skinned devils could be.

So, Cort, at the moment, wasn't too worried about his helper. The men from the ship weren't due for another four or five days yet, and Red Calf might have heard night signals unknown to white men, even one like Cort, indicating that a tribal dance or "sing" was in progress, following a successful foray over into Arizona.

Cort went first up among the nearby rocks to the pack mules. They dozed, well fed on the grain he brought back from Tucson, and the sky told him that the time was past midnight. The rocks that walled in the stream on either side and helped to hide his camp only threw out darker shadows from the faint crescent overhead. Cort slipped to the sandy floor again, and then a moving shadow caught his eye. He froze and waited. That faintly discernible shadow coming toward him was an Apache, and you never knew when one of the red devils, loaded up on too much *mescal* or *tequilla* which they got from the Mexicans, might slip in, and slit your throat with a knife in order to loot and then boast to impress some dark, exotic young maiden.

The shadow came on, approached the camp, paused. Then came a soft but far reaching *"Hoo-hoo."*

It was not the hoot of an owl. It was the sound the Apaches made while gigging their ponies along and digging at them with moccasined heels. It was Red Calf, seeing the empty blankets and signaling to him.

Red Calf knew about that .44 beneath Cort's pillow and

8

that the white man who employed him was a light sleeper and a deadly shot.

"Aqui," Cort answered in Spanish.

The Indian came forward and glided into the shadows. He spoke no English; nor had Cort, after years as a border-man, been able to master more than a few words of Apache. They spoke Spanish, Cort fluently, the Indian harshly, gutturally, broken.

He came up to Cort, slim and lithe; a man who might have been twenty-three or thirty-five. It was hard to tell the age of one of these wild Apaches. Cort had found him one day two years before, crawling along a rocky trail, a bullet squarely through his belly; dying of thirst. He could still remember that sinewy hand reaching for a knife, the man's beady black eyes looking up at him without fear; the eyes of a cornered animal who knew he was about to be killed.

Red Calf was one Apache the hard-riding, frustrated soldiers hadn't missed.

It wasn't until Cort had taken off his gun belt and un-slung a pack from a mule and brought out a canteen, that the fire in the black eyes had died. The grip on the knife handle had relaxed as Jim Cort, smuggler, cut away the dirty shirt and did a crude job of bandaging the wound.

Just how the Apache had ever managed to survive that long distance slug still lodged somewhere in his entrails, Jim Cort would never know. But Red Calf had survived . . . another reason for the loyalty.

He came closer to Cort. He wore an old, floppy hat and a long, ragged black coat, both probably the property of some unfortunate rancher, now dead. His loins carried a breech clout. Buckskin leggings covered his legs to above the knees, and he wore moccasins. That bare expanse of skin from about the knee of his thighs never seemed to bother Red Calf when the night air of the mountains

9

found him on the trail, coming to or going from old Tucson.

"They come," he said, and pointed back down the river.

"Who?" rapped out Cort sharply.

"My four brothers with men from big boat."

Cort unconsciously felt himself relax, and again the thought struck him that he'd been growing a bit taut recently. It was always that way, he guessed, when a man was making his last trip. Smuggling was fast becoming more dangerous every day. The soldiers up at Ft. Huachuca were making things tough. The fort had been erected over there in 1877 in order that the calvary might have a two-way shot at cutting off marauding Apaches breaking away from the reservation, sweeping south, and then streaking into Old Mexico to join their red brethren down there temporarily. And with the desert being combed more and more by those dusty, clanking cavalry patrols, the flow of alien Chinese, 'dobie dollars, silks, emeralds, and other commodities so dear to the people who could pay and ask no questions had been valved a bit.

The timid smuggler and the cautious, were disappearing. Only the bold—men like Jim Cort—were left. And Cort told himself that he was quitting. He had never bothered with such a thing as alien Chinese—he didn't believe in it. It was against his principles. But when it came to 'dobie dollars, silks, and emeralds . . . he remembered the burning desire, the bitterness that had engulfed him all these lonesome years, and he salved his conscience with the thought that if he didn't bring in what people wanted, then somebody else would.

He was still remembering Neely Anderson, the way she laughed at him, and he knew he was a fool to harbor such juvenile thoughts.

True, there was still a big stream of contraband flowing

10

across the border into the Territory. Bold, flamboyant, swaggering Lon Pearson and his raiders were still in the business, staging their cattle raids, their masked hold-ups of stages, their killing of other smugglers and seizure of pack trains. Bold Lon, who with his men swaggered into saloons and gaming houses and flouted their wealth and strength in the faces of timid lawmen. Lon was still operating. He who had lost one man and another had been shot through an arm when Cort's saddle horse and one fast mule outran them through an ambush.

Then, too, there was vicious old man Clanton with his brood of equally vicious sons. One of them, Billy, at eighteen was to lose his life in the OK corral in a new silver boom camp called Tombstone, in a shootout with the Earp brothers and Doc Holiday—a shootout that was to cost Billy and the two McLowry brothers their lives.

Even old man Clanton and his vicious sons had inadvertently helped Captain Hardy's soldiers by ambushing a Mexican pack train and killing more than twenty men in it.

No doubt about it, Cort thought, the smuggling business was getting tough; and the thought of Hardy brought back the bitterness to his lips as he heard the first sounds of the oncoming flatboat. It took him back six years to a certain big town back East and a girl named Neely Anderson he had tried so hard to forget.

Hardy had said there in the desert just four weeks before, eying the single big gray pack mule Cort was bringing back from Tucson:

"Not a thing in it, Jim, so it's too bad we didn't get you when you went North. But don't worry, my boy; the Army is slow but it wins out. I'll get you yet."

"Just a mule I picked up up North," Cort had answered harshly, looking sardonically at the ring of dusty soldiers surrounding him. "Taking him South to trade."

"Indeed, Jim?" with much sarcasm.

11

"Your boys look a little gaunted, Bert. You too. What do you lads think of Geronimo now?"

A hard, dark, almost savage frown crossed the ambitious face. "We'll get him. Don't you worry about that. We'll get him. And we'll get you, too, Jim. Too bad a man with your gentlemanly upbringing and education couldn't have chosen a better profession than smuggling."

Cort had let that one go by with a hard, taciturn grin acoss his lean, unhaven face. "If you mean my resigning from West Point after a year because I happen to be a man who is free and can't take Army discipline, had I any regrets concerning my decision, they'd all be swept away at sight of you. No thanks, Bertie, I'll stick to prospecting and a few other things."

He had ridden on through them, after their thorough search of his pack outfit, and the words that floated after him seared themselves into his brain for weeks afterward.

"I'll be glad to tell Neely that when I see her in Tucson on my next leave, Jim! She posted me a letter from there last week. They've come West to live."

Jim Cort shook off the savage thoughts as the small, flat-bottomed boat worked its way out of the sluggish waters and grounded within thirty feet of his camp. Red Calf had gone to the fire, stirred up the coals, and thrown on dry brush from a big pile nearby. The brush blazed brightly, and into the light of the fire came several men; four vicious-looking Apaches, brothers of Red Calf; a small, wiry-looking Mexican, and the most extraordinary white man Cort had ever seen.

He was a seaman but he looked more like a pirate off the Spanish Main. A bloodthirsty, cut throat pirate. And he smelled almost as odorously as the four beady-eyed, sullen-looking Apaches.

He stood a good six feet four inches, and his giant frame showed him to be a mass of knotty muscles. He was dressed in a dirty rag for a headpiece, a sleeveless leather

12

jacket laced with thongs up the front, ragged knee breeches, and a pair of heavy leather boots of a kind Cort had never before seen. His bare forearms, huge and iron hard, were covered with weird-looking tattooes that must have won respect from the four Indians. Had his beard and mustache been soaped and rinsed clean, they would have come out the color of corn silk.

He wore two pistols and three wicked-looking knives in a four-inch leather belt around his waist.

"Ahoy!" he boomed in a voice in keeping with his size.

He got out of the boat and came toward the fire, carrying two duffel bags.

"Who're you?" Cort asked curtly.

"Sailor Morton, mate! First mate on the four-master *Sally Ann,* just in from the China Seas."

He advanced to the fire, put down the two duffel bags very gently, and warmed his hands near the blaze, his great figure throwing grotesque shadows on the rocks back of them. Cort ignored him and looked at the Mexican, a question in his eyes. The Mexican was a slim, wiry, intelligent-looking man with a flowing black moustache: Garcia, former officer—and probably deserter—from the Mexican Army, *segundo* to Velasquez, with whom Cort did business.

Garcia mostly always came on these trips.

"What's he doing here?" Cort rapped out in Spanish. "Where's Velasquez?"

The sailor swung on him with a hard eye, his yellow teeth showing a grin through the beard.

"I speak it, mate," he boomed. "It and four other languages, with a smattering of Chinese, Malay, Russian, and a few words of Arabic, picked up in ports all over the world. Velasquez, you say? Where is he? At his headquarters down on the coast. But don't worry about your goods. They're all here. With something else I brought along. I'm going to help you deliver 'em, too."

13

He laughed in a bull-throated roar at Cort's hard, questioning look. Red Calf came up and spoke, with a nod at his four brothers.

"They are waiting," he said.

Chapter Two

CORT NODDED and said to Garcia, "I'll be back in a few minutes. Have the Indians unload."

He disappeared into the night, climbing up among the rocks. Up there he swung off around the side of a hill, then cut back and faded into the yawning jaws of a steep, rocky-walled canyon. Not even Red Calf knew where his cache was, though there was little doubt in Jim Cort's mind that the Apache trailer could easily have found it. But that bullet was still somewhere among his entrails, he was alive because of the man who hired him, and it was said that an Apache never forgot a friend, never forgave an enemy. Cort was a friend, word of him had spread along the border, and every Indian down there knew where his camp was hidden. Cort's danger always had lain in the chance that a few renegades might raid his camp, or one of those who knew him would be crazed with liquor.

He came back half an hour later, carrying a heavy gunny sack in one hand and a buckskin bag in the other. The buckskin bag was by far the heavier because it contained gold. Minted double eagles.

The four brothers of Red Calf looked at the gunny sack

14

and licked their lips as Cort placed it on the ground, skinned down the top, and brought forth two demijohns of really good whiskey. He always bought the best Tucson had to offer. He handed over the two jugs.

He didn't feel any too good over such dealings, but whiskey and money were what they wanted for guaranteeing the safety of the boats up the *Rio de la Concepcion*— River of Conception—from the Gulf of California. They had wanted guns too—those big single shot 45-70 Springfields of the kind the cavalrymen carried on their saddles, but to this demand he had adamantly said no. He wanted the blood of no ranchers and cowpunchers on his hands.

The four Apaches took the jugs and began to chatter among themselves as they uncorked, took huge swigs, and then gave Red Calf a drink. He took one, but Cort's helper drank little, surprising as it seemed. Nevertheless, Jim Cort shook his head as his helper handed back the demijohn.

"No more, Red Calf," he said in Spanish. "We leave with the mules at daybreak on the trails to Tucson."

The four Indians moved out, gone like shadows, and as silently. Cort knew that in a few more hours, just about daylight, things would start popping in the Apache's hidden camp back in the mountains. Geronimo was there— Cort had talked with him there just two days before, with Red Calf as interpreter—and the man who was driving cavalry generals frantic and their men to exhaustion probably would be the first to get a shot at one of the jugs.

"Whew!" grunted Sailor Morton when they were gone. "I've seen some bloody-looking pirates—Arab murderers, mulatto garroters, the scum of the earth in those ports— but none like them. Glad I got here. I wouldn't have gone back anyhow."

"Who told you you could go on?" Cort asked curtly. "Why *are* you here, mister?"

The sailor's booming laugh rolled out again. "I jumped

15

ship down the coast to see Velasquez. No more walking the decks for Sailor Morton. I asked him to send me to you."

"Why?"

"Ho-ho! Why, he asks! You'll see, mate."

Cort ignored him and turned to Garcia and spoke to him in Spanish. The Mexican nodded and indicated the bales of goods piled up close by the fire. He took from his coat pocket an oilskin packet and removed a paper. He handed it to Cort and they began working through the goods, checking each item.

It was all silk this time. Bolt after bolt of lustrous Chinese silk was unwrapped and inspected. Velasquez was a pretty fair man in his dealings, but you never could tell when he might slip in goods soiled or discolored by salt water. Cort examined each bolt. Flaming red and glittering blue colors met the eye; yellows and greens and white softer to the touch than a ball of cottonwood "fuzz" of the kind that floated down to the ground in the spring.

It was all there, enough for five light, compact packs which, if trouble broke, would enable the mules to put on plenty of speed. It lay there on the sand, a fortune in silk. It had been woven six thousand miles away, brought down to the great rivers, loaded on junks and sampans, and carried to Shanghai and Hong Kong, where the wharves teemed and the great fourmaster sailing ships lay at anchor with canvas lashed down and the smell of the ocean in the riggings. Then across the stormy Pacific to the coast of Mexico, where the rich Velasquez's schooners took off their share of the cargo and brought some of it north, into the Gulf of California to the mouth of the *Rio de la Concepcion*. Here some of the smugglers, working into California past San Diego, met and loaded. Cort's goods came up the river by the flat-bottomed boat. Where the stream forked, the Mexican crew, except for Garcia, left it, giving the oars to four Indians who had waited, sometimes for days. And

16

then another destination, and the goods were unloaded by a fire where a lean, saturnine-faced man with too many memories of the past waited . . . with American gold. In the cold of the next day's dawn, loaded on bobbing backs of speedy pack mules, it would start its final journey to Tucson; to Johannes Bruckmann, who answered no questions as he sold it to the dressmakers, the stores, the homes of the rich, where it would cling snugly to milady's white skin.

Cort nodded his satisfaction, checked the amount with Garcia, and tossed the bill of lading into the fire. He sat down on a rock, spread the saddle blanket beside him into a square on the sand, and began counting out gold. The pile grew and grew and Sailor Morton's eyes glittered unseen as he watched.

"Got any more of that around, mate?" he asked in a strangely soft voice.

Cort didn't reply. He and Garcia were putting the coins back in the sack once more. Cort looked at the Mexican.

"How is business at the schooner?" he asked.

Garcia shrugged. "Not very good, Jim. Many of the men who meet us have been caught crossing into the California country. Others have become frightened by the soldiers and have quit. We'll lay offshore for another two or three weeks and wait. But I hope they show up soon. Our rice supply might run out."

"Chinese?"

A nod. "Sixty of them, chattering like monkeys and smelling worse than the Indians." His black eyes narrowed speculatively. "Why don't you take them off our hands, Jim? A tremendous profit for you. You would have a much better chance up this far East, because the men who have been running them in work through the coast route to Los Angeles, San Francisco, and See-attle. There the patrols are much thicker. Take them, Jim. Let us bring them to your camp in flat-boats. Think of the profits!"

17

"It's too bad Sailor Morton don't know his navigation across the desert," boomed out the big man. "I'd bring the swabs up here in a hurry, and then slit their throats and bury them in the sand when the sojers hove in sight."

Cort looked at the bearded face, the two pistols and the knives in the broad leather belt. A cut-throat, if ever there was one.

"There's a thing called principle, even with a smuggler like myself," he said coolly. "We need settlers over in the Territory, but we need white men—not pigtailed coolies who'll work for thirty cents a day and rice."

He said to Garcia, "Did Lon Pearson or any of his men show up at the boat? No? I didn't expect it. He's more of a raider now." And he told of the attempted ambush.

Garcia said, "I'm sorry. I never liked him."

He rose with the bag of gold, and the immobile Red Calf went with him to the boat to help shove off. He would float downstream to the fork and there pick up his waiting men for the return trip to the mouth of the river. He waved good-bye, poled out from the sandy shore, and presently the hull cleared sand.

Only two men knew the location of the camp, besides the Sonora Indians, who never came. Garcia and Velasquez. Now there were three. Now there was Sailor Morton.

Jim Cort didn't like it.

He came back to the fire. Red Calf had put on more wood. Cort looked at the huge man who still stood facing it, warming his hands, the two duffel bags on the ground beside him. Apparently the few belongings he possessed.

"And now, sir," Jim Cort said to the man, "whatever you have to say, do so. You were not invited to this camp. Neither you nor any other man, besides those here tonight and Velasquez, is welcome. I travel alone. I have no friends, no companions except my Indian helper here. At day break we're leaving for the North, a trip of about five days. We travel by night after crossing the border. We travel light because of the necessity of speed sometimes. I can't leave you here because I don't want you in this camp either now or when I'm absent. Nor would I leave you otherwise. Within forty-eight hours after I did so, the dozens of Apaches who have seen the boat but never come to this camp would be dividing your belongings amongst themselves, leaving what was left of you for the coyotes and the buzzards. So you'll go with us, because I have no other choice in the matter. If trouble breaks with renegade Apache raiders down from the reservation, with a cavalry patrol from Fort Huachuca, or with Lon Pearson and his raiders, you are solely on your own. I assume no responsibility for your safety. In fact, I don't care a fig what happens to you, sir."

Sailor Morton began to haw-haw, and a good fog-horn coming into the Golden Gate at San Francisco on the Barbary Coast couldn't have been heard much farther.

"Now there's a matey after me own heart! I'd do the same fer you aboard a windjammer. I'd tear the guts out of you scrubbing a deck and send you up the rigging when the wind was howling like a banshee and the old tub's masts rolling forty degrees. And if we had to take to the long-boats, you'd be the last one in. Shake on it!"

He thrust out a paw with a grip of iron in the fingers and then sat down on a rock beside Cort.

"Listen, Cort," he said seriously. "You don't think I'd jump a good ship like the *Sally Ann* and come through this God-forgotten country just to get to the States again, do you? You don't think I'd ride up a river and a creek with a bunch of murderin', stinkin' Apache Indians as you'd cut a man's throat fer a sou to see new lands, do you? I saw you last year at Velasquez's headquarters, and I says, 'There's my laddie. That's the johnny fer Sailor Morton.' But I needed time. One more trip back to Hong Kong to collect fer the big pile of opium I smuggled in fer a Chinee merchant. He paid off, too. I got 'em!"

He reached up inside the leather-thonged coat and his big hand brought forth a soft leather sack. He opened it and a stream of stones reflected back a thousand green lights in the flickering illumination of the fire.

"Emeralds," the sailor said sonorously.

Chapter Three

THEY WERE a green, blinding, dazzling stream. He poured them back into the sack caressingly, and then again let them slide into a horny palm as though loving their touch.

"Emeralds," he said again, softly, and looked at Cort. His eyes, however, were glittering.

Cort took one of the green stones and looked at it, examining it closely. The others lay in Sailor Morton's great paw. Colors hit the firelight, were reflected, and just for a moment it seemed that the rocks, the fire, the very night blackness surrounding them appeared to take on a green hue. Red Calf stood motionless.

"Don't that blasted Indian *ever* set down?" grunted the sailor.

"Sometimes. He can rest standing. He can also run a wild desert horse down and capture it by jogging after it day and night until it plays out." Cort reached into a pocket of his shirt and brought forth a small magnifying glass. He said, squinting, as though quoting from a jeweler's book on precious stones: "A gem of pure green color. It is silicate of aluminum and a rare element known as beryllium. Only rubies and diamonds are considered more valuable. They are supposed to be either round or prismatic, with about six sides. Gravity is, for an average, approximately two and sixty-seven hundredths. They originally came from Egypt and Ethiopia."

He returned the stone, put away the magnifying glass. The sailor sat with the bag in one hand, astonished.

"Well, I'll be blowed," he ejaculated. "Velasquez said you were the sharp boy. I showed 'em to him because I knew you were smuggling diamonds and rubies too when he could get 'em; and, matey, you shoulda seen that hombre's eyes pop out like black buttons. He begged and wheedled, squeezin' his fat hands together till the palms squashed out like the belly of a red herring. But I wouldn't sell because I knew you'd probably get 'em anyhow. I brought 'em to you. Direct from Hong Kong."

"And with the blood of a hundred or a thousand men on them, too, no doubt."

"Aw, now wait a minute, Cort! You got more brains, than to be superstitious. Sure, they got blood on 'em. So's the gold you paid Garcia. Men died fer that gold— when they was washin' it out of the sands in California in '49, when it was took off stages by road agents, when it was lost over card tables an' follered by a knife in a slit throat. Now it's good minted U.S. coin. Men have always died fer anything of value. There's blood on it all. Sure, there's blood in these. The boys on board got wind I had somethin'. Our stern wasn't hard down under the horizon from Hong Kong before a scum tried to knife me in me cabin. I fixed him plenty, I did. Shoved him through a porthole fer shark meat after I slit his gullet, and that captain don't know to this day *exactly* w'at happened. We hit a breeze comin' around the Pacific circle and the old man laid on all the canvas she'd hold and let *Sally* run before the wind. And run she did, Cort. We made the west coast of Mexico five days ahead of sailing time. It was these gems. They brought us luck. How much?"

"Not interested," Cort lied. It was the smuggler in him now speaking.

"How much?" insisted the sailor.

"Not interested, I told you. It's time to turn in."

"Look here, Cort," wheedled Sailor Morton. "I want to get back to the states with gold in my pockets. I hear a lot about this Arizona Territory. Gold and silver by the ton; gambling and beautiful women. Ahhh . . . that's fer me. You don't know what it is to appreciate a woman of any color, size or age till you've trod a deck fer two months an' seen nothing but men an' sharks. These gems are worth a fortune. You take the profits you can get in the states. I want the feel of gold in me pockets when I hit across the line to the Territory."

They made the deal: forty-five thousand dollars in gold. Twenty-two hundred and fifty double eagles at twenty dollars apiece.

Morton got up and went to his duffel bags, bringing out a bottle of rum. He swigged lustily, sighed, wiped his dirty beard, and offered the bottle to Cort, who shook his head.

"Time to turn in," the smuggler said, rising.

"Hey, don't I get my money?" The sailor laughed protestingly.

"Not until the morning. Gold *and* emeralds might prove too great a temptation to a man who seems to be pretty good at slitting throats with a knife."

"Cripes, matey, I wouldn't try that on you."

Cort was at his blankets. He sat down to remove his moccasins again. He looked at the sailor, and then over to where Red Calf was getting between his own blankets.

"I know you wouldn't," he said evenly. "That Apache sleeps like a cat and is just about as fast. If you make a move tonight, Morton, you'll find out that the Indians also know a little about slitting gullets. Leave your guns and

22

knives over there on top of that rock. Make your bunk twenty feet away. You'll get your gold before daybreak in the morning."

"Haw-haw! So you don't trust me, eh?"

"Just about as far as I could throw one of those pack mules by the ears. Good night."

They got under way just at daybreak. Red Calf rode ahead, leading the way on a blanketed Indian pony that wasn't much looks but bred to the desert. Cort followed, leading the string of five pack mules, loaded with bolts of silk, the emeralds now nestling inside his shirt. He had been lucky in having the gray mule, much bigger than the others, which he'd bought in Tucson. On it Sailor Morton brought up the rear astride an improvised blanket saddle Red Calf had rigged for him. There hadn't been a sack big enough or strong enough to hold the huge pile of gold coins, until Red Calf cut open his big burro-skin water bag at one end and gave it to him. The sack, awkward to hold, was now in front of the man from the sea, across the big gray mule's withers. It made a pretty heavy load for the mule, but the sailor stubbornly had refused Cort's suggestion that he put the gold in a pack. Now Morton brought up the rear and swore salty oaths about every time the gray mule's feet touched the ground. He had no stirrups to help ease the weight off his seat. Red Calf, being an Indian, didn't need any.

The Mexican desert stretched away in all directions into hazy distance too far for the naked eye to see; hot, sullen, resentful; greasewood and yucca-studded. It drove northward to where, far in the haze, the *Oro Blanco Montes*— the White Gold Mountains—thrust sun-baked ridges and humps into the desert sky. That was Arizona Territory over there across the line beyond the haze, and there they would camp for a few hours.

It was a desolate land of heat, a land of death, a land of renegade Apaches on raiding sprees off the San Carlos

23

Reservation; a land where furtive-eyed horsemen holed up in gullies and arroyos and kept lookouts on high vantage points to warn of all comers. Here and there along creeks little settlements flourished, motley collections of 'dobie shacks the occupants of which were mostly males. The few female inhabitants were Mexicans, the dark-haired women of those who rode mostly by night.

The pack train moved on across the desert as the sun went higher. It was overhead now, throwing its steaming rays down upon the three riders and the plodding pack mules. Red Calf rode stolidly to the fore, his black eyes scouring every knoll, every bush, every gully. Back of the train Sailor Morton hitched at his heavy money bag across the withers of the gray mule, wiped sweat from his streaming brow, and swore at everything in sight.

Of the three, Cort seemed to be the least affected. For this, he told himself, was his last trip. Johannes would give him a good twenty thousand profit on the emeralds. The years of danger as a borderman were coming to an end. She had laughed at him that night when he had returned from West Point, where Upper Classman Hardy was finishing his last year; the jeering laughter had flamed in her carefree blue eyes; she had laughed hard when he had asked her to marry him and come West.

"Profligate," was the word she had used.

And that had hurt. It had cut deep, seared him. It had burned the harder when she reminded him that he wasn't a man at all. He had first spent his inheritance and then thrown away a good career in the Army for the pleasures of the cabarets.

Of course, she had been young then, only eighteen; the daughter of rich parents—her father was a financier. But when a man is young the hurt can cut deep in tender years, and now, though he had hardened, the shell was on the outside. The hurt was still within. A scar, and a kind of grim determination, had kept him going all these years.

24

He had wanted money so he could come back to her and flaunt it in her face.

Childish, he had told himself a thousand times during the past six years. It was terribly childish to let a young girl's scorn put a scar on a man's heart.

Thought of what he had been brought a half-smile to his face, more of a quirk of the lips. He unconsciously looked down at the boots, spurs, the sheathed .44 that had killed three men, and compared this older Jim Cort with the younger James Van Cortland. There wasn't much to compare.

A grimace crossed his hard, taciturn face. Jim Cort, killer of three men in gun flights, suspected smuggler and badman, with a name along the toughest stretch of the border from Corpus Christi to San Diego.

The horse beneath him plodded on beneath the sun. The pack mules slobbered and kept slack rein. Up ahead Red Calf rode on, watching, scanning. And for some strange reason Cort knew in that moment that it didn't mean anything any more. He had, in a flash, outgrown it.

So she was in Tucson with her family?

All right, let her stay there. He had outgrown it now; the desert years had hardened him. He had come out of it a man. Perhaps not the type some people would have considered the epitome of what a real man should be. But Cort shrugged that off. A man's fight must first be with himself. The fight had lasted six hard years in the desert, and he knew now he had won.

Sailor Morton jolted up beside him, cursing again as he hitched at the heavy sack of gold coins in front of him, trying to keep it balanced on the withers of the big gray mule.

"Well, you wanted it," Cort grunted sourly. "You got it."

"How much longer, matey? Blow me, but my thighs on the inside feel like they've been scraped by a shark's teeth. And the blasted sun is puttin' my eyes out. Now I know why you cow wrastlers wear big hats. How much further?"

25

"Not much. The *Oro Blancos* are there in the distance. We'll camp for a few hours and wait until dark to go on."

The sailor grunted painfully and dropped to the rear again. The train wound on, working along the winding trails, dipping in and out of gullies, and crossing ridges—but not until Red Calf signalled that all was clear.

Early in the afternoon they reached the *Oros*. They had swung a bit to the east to avoid crossing Papago country. The Papagos were friendly enough, but Government agents weren't. It was best to stick to the wild, barren country. They came at last to a kind of promontory, climbing it, but kept off the skyline. There was a big spring about two miles ahead where Cort planned to camp. Apache Springs, it was called. Red Calf went up the slope ahead to take a look, *hoo-hoo*-ing his pony with digs of moccasined heels. He swung down, crawled up, and then Cort saw him duck back. His arm went up in a signal.

"Oh, oh," called out Morton. "The bloody pirate's seen something."

He rode up and Cort handed him the reins of the lead pack mule. "Wait here. I'll go up for a look. We may have to run for it. And shoot it out."

"Who do you reckon?"

"Anybody. Soldiers from the fort on patrol, renegade Apaches off the San Carlos Reservation, Lon Pearson and his raiders trying another ambush on me. I warned you, Morton. If there's trouble it's every man for himself."

"I heard you the first time," grunted the sailor, taking the reins and twisting painfully in the improvised "saddle."

Cort gigged his horse up among the scattered greasewoods, sand and gravel rattling beneath its hoofs. He pulled up alongside Red Calf's pony, swung down, removed his hat and crawled up beside where the Indian lay. Red Calf pointed silently.

Down in the next draw, about a quarter of a mile to the east, mounted figures flashed out of sight in the thicker,

26

greener brush, flashed up again, disappeared into another gully. Then came shots, the bawl of a cow in pain, and Red Calf looked at Cort and grinned the nearest thing to a wide grin possible in an Apache. Cort understood. The Government hadn't been too good about keeping its word with the Indians when it came to the matter of food. Grand old Cochise, who had died not too long before, had let his people go hungry for days to keep his word to white men who hadn't kept theirs.

Now it appeared that a raiding party was off the reservation. They had just run down and shot a cow.

"Your people?" Cort asked in Spanish.

Red Calf shook his head. *"De la reservacion Yanqui.* From the Yankee reservation.

Renegades.

Cort lay there, pondering his next move. Had they been Sonora Apaches, Red Calf's outfit, he would have no cause for apprehension. But renegades were different. The pack train might prove too tempting.

It was then that Red Calf pointed again, toward the west, where a thin streamer of dust was rounding another promontory about a mile away.

"Soldados," the Indian said.

Jim Cort didn't have to be told. The dust shape was all too familiar. A cavalry patrol from Fort Huachuca. Cort lay there and cursed under his breath. The Indians were to the east of them, the patrol coming in from the west. They were caught almost between the two.

Cort slid down and rose to his feet, putting on his hat. His natural instinct was to turn and make a run south for it. But suppose the hungry raiders now working over the slaughtered cow also chose to run south, with the soldiers in pursuit? They might all be brought up together in one honey of a mixup. Yet if they ran *north,* the patrol would be sure to see them.

So Cort crawled up to the crest again and waited.

27

Sailor Morton came scrambling up on foot, panting and sweat-streaked. "I had to get off that blasted mule fer at least a minute or two," he panted. "What's up?"

"Where are the pack mules?" snapped Cort.

"Tied to a bush. What's up?" he repeated.

Cort had unslung his glasses now. He focused them on the mouth of the gully. The Indians had dragged the cow back down to the mouth, possibly to where they could keep a sharp lookout. There were about a dozen of them, and the glasses brought them up close. They were sawing and hacking away, taking off big chunks of fresh, dripping beef. One of them had a fire going, but others were eating it raw; eating it ravenously. They could live on jackrabbits, lizards, even rattlesnakes; but they evidently had ridden far and hard or the raiding had been poor. They were hungry.

Cort told the sailor, swinging around to view the oncoming soldiers.

"So we're caught between 'em, eh?" asked the sailor. "And now it's every man for himself."

"Get back to the mules—and you'd better cache that gold someplace. It looks like we'll have to ride, and ride like blazes."

"Right."

Morton slid back down the slope again to the pack train and Cort once more turned his attention to the problem at hand, pondering their next move.

He and Red Calf waited.

Chapter Four

THE RAIDING PARTY were still busy gulping food in big chunks. Through the glasses Cort could see a buck stick a huge chunk of beef into his mouth, hold the rest with one hand, and saw off the bite in front of his lips. They wore varicolored cloth headpieces, motley coats and shirts, a couple had on Levis, and all wore leggings and moccasins. Their bunched horses looked pretty good, probably the result of a night foray against the herds of some San Pedro or Santa Cruz River rancher.

Cort looked at Red Calf. The Indian had a carbine slung to his pony. He could signal them with a shot. But Apaches were a strange people in many ways. These raiders were *Yanquis,* not their own people; nor would it have made any difference probably. It was this element in their makeup which caused them to hire out to the soldiers as Apache police to help trail and run down members of their own tribe and even of their families. For a period of one year, as police, they trailed mercilessly, fought mercilessly, and shot mercilessly. The moment the tenure of service ended they faded back in the hills to join those they had hunted, taking with them every gun and every round of ammunition they could steal. By that time many of those they had hunted had become police, and the tables were reversed. The hunted became the hunter. The former police became the fugitives. It was a game they loved, an opportunity to ride and fight, and woe to the man who lost. It was none of their business that these strange *Yanquis* wanted to catch Geronimo because old Cochise had been old and foolish and peaceable. The pay was good, and there was an opportunity to steal guns and ammunition.

Red Calf made no move to warn the busily gorging raiders.

"Do you know any of them?" Cort asked in Spanish, handing over the powerful binoculars.

The Indian took them, squinted, made adjustments on the lenses, and finally nodded.

"Yes. There is Deer Tail, a very bad Indian from the reservation. He is a minor chief and is their leader. He is one of Geronimo's men. They are going to join him now."

"They'll join a lot of their brothers in the Happy Hunting Grounds in a few minutes unless they get going," Cort grunted. "Hardy's men are coming closer. Why don't they see them?"

"They will find out. Let them fight."

It was indeed unusual for wild Apaches, even after life on the reservation, to be so incautious. Cort guessed it was because ravenous hunger had temporarily dulled their instinct for danger. He let it go at that. There was going to be one beauty of a fight, and it was just possible that, during the confusion, he could get his pack train away unseen.

It took another half-hour. By now the soldiers were close enough so that Cort, hidden among the greasewoods at the top of the ridge, could make out quite clearly the features of Captain Hardy in the saddle. Hardy, old friend of the past, who had been finishing up at West Point the year Cort entered. He'd done quite well, no doubt about that. Promotions usually were pretty slow, tedious affairs . . . coming up from second lieutenant to first, and then to captaincy.

But Cort knew Hardy, a stern disciplinarian who fol-

30

lowed the rules with the passion of a man who loved the rule book and the Army.

Finally Cort turned to Red Calf. "It's time to get out of here. If we get in trouble, you run for the camp. Don't fight and don't get shot. Do not fire on the soldiers. Understand?"

Before the Indian could nod a reply, a sharp, shrill yell cut the air from down below to the east of them; an Apache yell of warning. Turbanned figures sprang into life, leaping for horses. A bugle blew. The cavalry column broke into a hard run, and so did Jim Cort. He leaped for his horse, spurred down the slope, rounded the corner where the train had been.

It was gone!

Sailor Morton had taken him at word. In case of trouble, it was *every man for himself* ...

Meanwhile, two evenings before, some kind of a military cyclone had hit the headquarters building in Fort Huachuca. Colonel Eblen—known among the junior officers as "The Old Man" and among the troopers as "Colonel Blunderbuss"—had called in Captain Lee Hardy. Hardy stood before him, thirty-one years of age, the perfect picture of the West Point-trained officer; military, erect, and with the certain deference junior officers are expected to cultivate when standing before their superiors.

The Old Man was pacing the floor of his office, a cigar puffing furiously beneath his cropped gray mustache. He wheeled, removed the cigar, and pointed it at Hardy from between a stubby index and second finger.

"I want results, Captain," he snapped. "Results, you understand? You've been in the service long enough to understand what a chain of commands mean. The brass hats in their plush offices in Washington are bellowing like a bull in a cow pen about Apache depredations we can't stop, road agents, smugglers, and anything else that seems to

31

come to their befogged minds. It's bad enough that the general now in command out here—and this is strictly off the record, Captain—spends most of his time lallygagging around trying to arrange a powwow with Geronimo, while at the same time he burns my shirt tail for not *catching* him! All I'm supposed to do with about four hundred troopers is keep the Apaches on the reservation, stop the Sonora Apaches from crossing the line to join them on more raids, listen to the bawls of the Indian agent, protect stages carrying gold and silver from road agents like this ruffian Lon Pearson and his men, be careful not to cross the Mexican line and ruffle the tail feathers of the Mexican government, maintain a fort with strict military discipline . . .

He let the rest of the words trail off into growls past the cigar once more clenched between his teeth. The colonel continued to pace the floor.

Hardy stood before him, at ease, and inwardly a little contemptuous. He was only a captain now, but he had come up fast. Once he got those major's oak leaves and then a full colonel's eagles on his shoulders, there would be no apoplectic outbursts like this.

Three passions consumed Captain Lee Hardy's life: promotion to a higher rank with its attendant responsibilities, wealth, and the winning of Neeley Anderson as his wife. They occupied most of his waking hours and even his dreams. He wanted them, he would get them. The blueprint for the future was laid out, and nothing would be allowed to stand in his way. Nothing!

It was a maddening beat in his brain. He knew what he wanted. He would get them because the three meant everything in his life. Neely, at twenty-four, was one woman in a thousand. She was worth it. Any struggle, any scarifice, any means. . . .

"Yes, sir," he said.

The colonel sat down back of his desk again. Something

like a sigh, the sigh of a tired old man about to retire, came whistling out of his bulbous nose.

"Captain Hardy," he said, "this whole country is making fools of the cavalry. We're trained men. We're efficient. Many older officers are veterans of the war between the states. We know fighting according to orthodox tactics, we know hardships in the field, we know military discipline. But we go out after these murdering red devils and they fade away into the deserts and gullies like shadows. They simply disappear. They signal to each other with smoke miles away—miles before we can get there. We sneak up on them at night, a coyote yaps a couple of times, and they're gone again. We ride from daylight until dark—for what? To find the ashes of their campfire still warm; to make out a report to the brass hats that they've got away from us again. And all the time they're bellowing about results! So I want *results!*"

Hardy had stood listening to it all. He knew there was little use in speaking until the Old Man got the steam off his chest. Now he shifted his sabre and cleared his throat.

"Could the captain make a suggestion to the colonel, sir?" he inquired.

"What?" came back the snapped reply.

"A new tactic—a temporary one, sir. Admittedly, sir, the Apaches have it on us when it comes to stalking them on their own grounds, even with the help of native police whom I never trusted. We'll get them in time, sir—the Army always does. Meanwhile, this border is crawling with smugglers bringing in everything from jewels to alien Chinese. The big fellows, sir. The cunning ones. Men like this desperado who calls himself Jim Cort."

"Hmmm," commented the colonel. "Go on, Captain Hardy."

"You've heard of Cort, sir?"

"I've heard of him. Some kind of a lone wolf smuggler

33

and borderman. Educated. From back East, I believe. A former gentleman turned desperado. Clever man."

"Possibly because he spent a year at West Point, sir. I've known him since boyhood."

The colonel leaned forward. He placed the cigar butt in an ash tray on his desk. His eyes weren't angered now; they were interested. He knew this capable officer now standing before him.

"Go on," Colonel Eblen said quietly.

Hardy went on. "He was profligate, sir. Spent his inheritance, resigned from the Point because he didn't like military discipline. Got into trouble over a girl who refused to marry him on account of his drinking and carousing. Came West and turned bad. Killed three men in gun fights, sir."

"And?"

"I caught him twice, but he was on his way south from Tucson, and there was no evidence, as I wrote in my reports. But I know Cort—his real name is James Van Cortland, sir—and I know about where he makes his smuggling runs. So let us suppose that with the pressure on from Washington, we did get some of the results you asked for? If we could pull in a man like 'Jim Cort' and turn him over to the United States marshal for prosecution, it might, sir, temporarily relieve the pressure now being put on us." Hardy was careful to use the word "us". "In brief, sir, it might help to stop this—er—rash in Washington. So suppose that I take out a patrol with plenty of provisions, ostensibly to hunt Indians but in reality to get this Cort or any more of his kind. It would show *results*. One captured smuggler with his pack train would look better on the reports than half a dozen sullen Indians being returned under guard to the San Carlos Reservation."

Colonel Eblen got up. He relit the dead cigar. Then he looked at the younger man before him.

"Captain," he said levelly, "if you can bring me in just

34

one smuggler's pack train withtin the next week or ten days, so I can have something to show to the general, I'll recommend you for a major's commission and see that you get a two weeks' leave from duty."

"Yes, sir," Captain Lee Hardy replied.

He went out, smiling to himself, crossing the compound to the officers' quarters. A man owed a duty to the Army, but he owed one first to himself. Let the Indians raid. He had seen Cort four times on the trails, twice when he couldn't catch him, and twice when Cort was coming south with no evidence against him. That last time had been four weeks ago, when he had told the smuggler about Neely Anderson and her family being in Tucson. Hardy thought he knew his man. And the captain would, like a coyote hunter, the old time trappers, play on the habits of the hunted. Cort covered a thirty-mile-wide stretch of country on his trips to and from Tucson, taking different trails each time. But soldiers stationed on ridges in pairs could signal with mirrors or spur to camp with information. It might take a week, ten days, three or four weeks . . .

Hardy sent for his orderly and told the man to have Lieutenant Kester report. Kester arrived within fifteen minutes.

"Captain?" he inquired, saluting.

"Lietutenant," Hardy said to the slim young officer, "we're leaving at daybreak. I want twenty-four of the hardiest troops in the command, under Sergeant Toland. Hand-picked men. Provisions for three to four weeks. I've just seen the colonel, and he wants results. We're going to get them. We shan't come back until we do. Is that perfectly clear?"

"Perfectly, sir," replied the lieutenant. He threw another salute with a gloved right hand, stepped outside, and was gone.

Hardy began inspecting his equipment.

Chapter Five

THEY LEFT the fort just as daylight turned the silent darkness of the fort to gray; out of the silent compound, answering the sentry's challenge, dropping down the slope, the Fort Huachuca Mountains looming up bold and dark in back of them.

They swung due west and rode hard all day long, camping that night on the banks of the Santa Cruz River. At dawn of the following day they crossed, hit the desert again, and drove on. Accoutrements rattled and squeaked. The horses' hooves rang out sharply on hard trails. Somewhere back of them came a song in trooper slang and with unprintable words as the trooper leading the heavily laden pack mules herded them along.

It was a hard outfit; a tough outfit, well heeled and able to take care of any situation that might come along. It was led by a brilliant officer with bars on his dusty shoulders, tall and wiry and hard in the saddle. Lieutenant Kester rode beside him, an intelligent young officer upon whom Hardy could depend. Sergeant Toland, middle-aged, potbellied, and crusty, was a top non-commissioned man who knew his business as well as he knew the desert. Toland had ridden with J.E.B. Stuart's men, saw the war lost, took his oath of allegiance to Lincoln's Government, and now was still in the Army he loved. Good men all.

They worked westward all that day, keeping a sharp

36

lookout for tracks. Kester was privately of the opinion they should have bought along two or three Apache police, but he knew Hardy and he had wisely said nothing. Hardy's contempt for the Indians, his distrust of them, probably stemmed from the fact that, when the final showdown came, white men must be accorded full credit.

That afternoon they pulled up to rest for a few minutes, drank thirstily from canteens, and stretched out saddle kinks. They hadn't found a single track worth following. North of them, miles away in the haze, were the creeks, the rivers, the little settlements without name. Places where smugglers stopped over among those of their kind. Hardy made a sudden decision. He turned to Lieutenant Kester.

"I've been over this country before. Not a watering place for miles ahead. We'll swing back and make camp tonight at Apache Springs. Just a hunch I'm playing."

They swung up into saddles and the patrol got under way once more. Hardy instinctively edged them south toward the escarpments of the distant foothills, where his men would have the advantage of cover. He thought he knew his man. There had been no tracks of a mule pack train in two days. That meant Cort would be coming along in a week, two weeks. . . .

They would proceed cautiously, play the waiting game with men in pairs strung out on high vantage points, and let the quarry fall into the trap.

Lieutenant Kester said nothing as they rode through periods of the day when they should have been resting. He knew Hardy. He was still thinking about it that afternoon when the captain threw up a gauntleted hand and brought the column to a halt. The sweaty mounts carrying dust-covered riders stopped. Captain Hardy turned to Lieutenant Kester. He pointed up ahead to where mouths of ominous-looking gullies and bold ridges showed in the distance.

"Noticed anything up there, Lieutenant?" he asked.

"Nothing, sir."

"Just a movement. Looked like riders."

"Apaches?"

"I don't know. They slid out of sight."

"Orders, sir?"

"We'll continue forward," Captain Hardy answered crisply. "They're Apaches, I believe. Slid out of sight too quickly. If we contact them, the troop will give chase. But we're out for bigger game this time."

Hardy started the column forward once more. Kester dropped back a pace, but not without the thought that it would have been better had they brought along some of the capable Apache police. Then he saw the distant haze of a smoke fire. Hardy was examining it through his glasses. They went on. A jackrabbit jumped up from beneath a greasewood, where it had dug a cool resting place in the shade, and went loping off out of sight. A buzzard sailed effortlessly in the sky, legs stretched out in the wind, repulsive red neck craning down in search of carrion. Hardy had been using his glasses again.

"About a dozen of the red devils, Lieutenant," he said. "Eating a butchered cow. I saw what I thought was movement atop one of the ridges. Probably one or two of their lookouts. Not much use trying to get around to cut them off. If they're heading for Mexico, they'll flee in that direction. If they get uneasy, they'll streak northward for the reservation again. We'll go straight in and try to run them down. Pass the word along to shoot and shoot to kill."

The dusty column broke into speed, the mule tender whipping his packed mounts along to keep up. They drove straight for the canyon mouth; and the Apaches, their usual instincts blunted by hunger, let them get to within a quarter of a mile or so before the first shrill yell of warning cut the air. It carried far across the desert, telling that the patrol had been discovered. Figures began scurrying, running toward blanketed horses, and the troopers bored in at a dead run, some beginning to shoot from the saddle. The sounds of the single-shot 45-70 Springfields broke out above the drum of running hoofs as the troopers with Hardy at their head tried to close in for the kill.

It was about then that, to the north, Captain Lee Hardy saw a slight movement, and not too far away. It was the tail end of a mottled black and white mule bobbing from sight down a draw. Hardy yelled a command to Sergeant Toland to pass on to Kester and wheeled away to the north, driving in the spurs. This was what he had been hoping for. Apaches didn't use mules when there was a good supply of horses handy. It might be a rider down there around the turn, but something about the bobbing rump told him it was a pack mule. He drove his cavalry mount forward with all the speed it could maintain.

Back of him the shouts were still sounding, growing fainter in the distance. Hardy forgot them in the mission ahead. He reached the turn in the gully where the mule's rump had disappeared, and a fierce, triumphant joy went through him at sight of the five running pack animals. He jerked his rifle free from its boot and began firing. He knew there was little chance of a hit while shooting from the back of a running horse; but his disappointment that the huge man leading them—a man with a rag around his head—was not Cort was alleviated by the knowledge, of which he was certain in his own mind, that the man was a smuggler.

"Halt!" he bellowed, just because it would look good on his report, and fired again.

The rider dropped the rope on the lead mule. They plunged off to one side to come to a confused halt while the man ahead, astride a huge gray mule, picked up more speed.

Hardy hauled his heaving mount to a halt. It was winded and trembling. He knew he could follow the man and eventually get him; and had it been Cort he would have

39

killed his mount in the effort. But the big man with the rag around his head was a stranger, and the pack mules were there off to one side. Captain Lee Hardy rode over, picked up the now dangling rope on the lead mule, his eyes surveying with satisfaction the five sweaty animals. No prospector's outfit, this. No supply train for riders in desert line camps or sheep herders working the wilds with their bands of woolies. This was it. His luck was with him.

The Old Man had wanted results.

Well, he was getting them! And Hardy knew in a moment of exultation that those oak leaves of a major already were as good as on his shoulders. He led the hard-panting animals back up the draw, rounded a corner, and came face to face with Jim Cort.

Cort's horse blocked the trail; Cort's hand was close by his thigh where the sheathed .44 rested. Captain Hardy came to a halt.

Jim said, "Hello, Bert." The full name was Albert Lee Hardy, but during their boyhood days back East it had always been Bert.

"Hello, Jim," Hardy said. "I see your hand close by your gun. You probably intend to make an attempt to recover your pack train. Don't do it."

"I didn't know you were chasing me, Bert," Cort answered sardonically. "I was so busy getting out of there when your men hit the Apaches that I didn't know *anybody* was chasing me."

Hardy recognized the sarcasm. It made his lips tighten. He realized now that his zeal, and a bit of bad luck, had caused him to defeat the very purpose he had set out to accomplish. Had he only waited, trailed the smuggler who had led the pack mules . . .

"Never mind the sarcasm," he snapped back. "I notice your horse is heaving a bit, as though he'd been running."

"It was time to run." Cort grinned at him.

"Or you could have been trying to catch up with your man."

"The only man I have," Cort answered truthfully, "is an Apache Indian helper I use for safe passage through this country, and sometimes as an interpreter."

"I know. I'm not a gambler, but I'd bet a month's pay that you even know where Geronimo is right at this moment."

"Don't make the bet." Cort advised him. "You might lose. I'm not saying, Bert, but it looks like you've made a haul."

Hardy had twisted around in the saddle, doing it gradually in the hope he could get open the flap of his holster. Cort saw the movement and his gray eyes went cold.

"Don't be a fool," he said sharply. "Don't try to throw that gun on me, Bert. I'd drop you cold."

"I've got men up there not far south. If they heard the shot you'd never leave this country alive."

Cort shrugged his slim, square shoulders. "You're the man who was going for his gun," he reminded the captain.

"I'll still go for it if you try to recover this pack train!"

"Possession nine points of the law, I believe," Cort answered dryly. "It looks like you've captured a pack train of contraband. Even though there are no witnesses present, and I could easily shoot you and take it, I wouldn't deny you the pleasure of making out a good report to the colonel and then, modestly, telling Neely about it when you see her again. Old school ties, you know. The Point and all that, even though you were an upper classman and I only a plebe."

Hardy's iron control gave way under the bitter sting of irony. "Damn you, Jim, I ought to arrest you and take you in," he said angrily.

"Try it," grinned Cort. "If you do, Bert you'll never live to make that report."

He gigged his horse on past Captain Hardy and the pack

train and rode on down the trail, leaving the fuming officer staring after him. "Good old Bertie." Cort grinned again, to himself. "I'd like to be watching through an open window when he tells Neely all about it."

He rode on, smiling sardonically. He did not look back.

Chapter Six

THE *Santa Cruz*—Sainted Cross—River is just east of the *Oro Blanco* Mountains and runs a course almost north and south toward Tucson, passing the old city just a bit to the west. It wasn't much of a river, even then. It was more a wet streak of sand, except during rainstorms, when the yellow waters hit the bends in a rage and tore gashes out of the sandy banks. It created bluffs, which were always crumbling, to a height of thirty feet.

It was back of one of these bluffs that Lon Pearson and his raiders had their little settlement.

The place consisted of about a dozen one- and two-room adobe shacks, set back in a grove of big cottonwoods. Here Pearson lived alone in the largest of the edifices. Scattered around in whatever locations took their fancy were the cabins of his men and their Mexican women. It was headquarters, where law was Lon Pearson's word and their six-shooters. There wasn't a sheriff within nearly two hundred miles, and this suited the raider and his men. On that score they had no complaints. From the settlement they rode out on forays, sometimes to steal horses from the ranchers, sometimes to rob stages, often to go into Tombstone, Bensen, and old Tucson to get drunk on the proceeds of a raid and toss their money over the gambling tables and to the feminine parasites who bestowed their temporary favors.

They had just held up the Bensen stage the day before, leaving one man behind. A man called "Pancho".

Pancho was the offspring of a wild Apache father and a Mexican mother, mingling native Mexican intelligence with the cunning of his father. He had lived with the Apaches and spoke his father's language as well as he did his mother's. He was the best trailer in the outfit, an asset Lon Pearson valued very much when they went out looking for smuggler pack trains. He could cover a trail as only an Apache could do it—hence the reason Pearson always left him behind. By the time a posse of befuddled citizens, outraged though they might be, arrived at the scene of a stage holdup, there simply were no tracks. Pancho had covered them.

Thus Lon Pearson awoke that afternoon about two o'clock and in a savage frame of mind. The holdup had netted but six hundred dollars from passengers, there being nothing in the strongbox. Nothing else of value except a couple of mail sacks, which the raider had been too intelligent to touch.

It had taken five men to pull the job, and the proceeds hardly had been worthwhile, certainly not in keeping with the risks involved. The five had played poker until four in the morning, and Pearson had lost his share to Pancho, the winner. Pearson didn't mind the loss of the money. It was the fact that, being a chronic drinker who kept a bottle alongside his bed and drank during waking spells, his nerves were on edge all the time. There was that constant strain of knowing that some day they'd run into a U.S. marshal, a patrol of soldiers, a night guard at one of the ranches, a decoy stage armed to the teeth with "passen-

43

gers," or a smuggler train guarded by men with carbines.

Pearson took a big swig out of a quart bottle and went outside to the wash basin on a bench beside the doorway. He soused his blond locks, straightened his wide-shouldered frame, and towelled his handsome face. There was a cracked mirror hanging from a nail driven into the adobe wall, and he surveyed his countenance with little satisfaction. His eyes were getting a bit bloodshot, he noted, and there was a slight puffiness beneath them of late. Only hard riding kept him, at twenty-nine, lean and hard. It was his one insurance against quickly going to seed.

He cooked a breakfast of bacon and flapjacks, lounged around under the cottonwoods, moodily reflecting that it was time to retire and settle down to an honest living. A man with his money ought to be able to buy a pretty good ranch along the river—something like the Batton place—and make it pay. They could still hold up an occasional stage, pick off a rich smuggler pack train, and sell the goods to Johannes Bruckmann for a fat profit.

Pearson was still thinking it over that afternoon when the stranger rode into camp aboard a big gray mule and pulled up right in front of where the outlaw leader sat whittling a piece of dry cottonwood stick. Lon Pearson stared at the newcomer. The latter slid to the ground, cursing salty oaths, and gave the gray mule a good kick in the belly to vent his spleen.

"Blow me!" he said disgustedly, and walked spraddle-legged toward the bench. He sat down painfully and stretched out his great legs with the rippling muscles, let go a sigh of relief, and completely ignored the man with the knife.

"Blow me, matey!" he said again.

"Who're you?" the outlaw leader asked curtly.

"Sailor Morton, matey just in from the China Seas. Wisht I'd stayed on the *Sally Ann*."

Pearson's eyes took in his great figure and dress, the two

44

pistols and three knives in the wide leather belt. He had never seen a man like this one.

"What are you doing here?"

Sailor Morton removed the rag around his head and used it to wipe away the sweat. He looked at the rag, not at Lon Pearson.

"It's a devil of a country," he remarked. "Every time you turn around somebody is asking what are you doing here. Like that bloke Jim Cort. I came into his camp—"

Pearson had tossed away the stick. He was all ears now. He said sharply, "Go on and tell it."

Sailor Morton told him. Pearson, realizing the man was weary, went inside and brought out the partly empty bottle. The sailor drank lustily, and finished his story.

"So that's how it is, matey. Them damn sojers hit the Indians an' this Jim Cort, the smuggler, said as how it was every man for himself. So I took the pack train and set full sails down the canyon. Figgered I'd sell the stuff and then come back and get my gold. Next thing I knowed this officer bloke with a rifle opens up on me an' I have to hit her in a full breeze with all sails set, leaving the cargo behind." He spat, drank from the bottle again, and looked at Pearson. Then his eyes roved around the clearing, saw the adobe shacks with their busy Mexican women. "This don't look like no sailors' mission in Singapore," he finished. "Now you do some talking."

"I'm Lon Pearson," the raider chief said, and told nothing more. "My men here are sort of traders. But I know your Jim Cort. Sixty Chinese, you say?"

"Ay."

"That's fine. We'll bring them in." He rose and let out a shout. "Oh, Smithy! Smithy, come over here!" He turned to the sailor. "Smith is my *segundo,* or second in command," he explained.

"I speak the language, matey," Sailor Morton said.

"Good. I'll send Smith—here he comes now."

Smith came at a fast walk through the shade of the cottonwoods. The Mexicans called them "Alamo" trees.

The *segundo* was short and bow-legged with a short black beard. He was in his forties.

"Smitty," Pearson said, "we've got a visitor here in Sailor Morton." The two men shook hands. "Garcia had sixty Chinese aboard a schooner in the Gulf, with no takers. I want you to get some of the boys and go after them. Garcia don't know you, so I'll have to give you a note to him. Tell him it's from Jim Cort and that he's changed his mind about those Chinese. He'll run them up the river on flat boats to Cort's camp. Morton here will show us where it is."

"Hold it, matey!" protested the sailor. "I wouldn't make that ride back again for all the Chinese in China."

"We've got a saddle you can use. Belonged to one of our men Cort killed a few weeks back when we tried to ambush him. You can make it. So Cort disappeared for thirty minutes to get the gold he paid you? Pancho can find his cache. We'll wait in Cort's camp, take his cache and delivery of the Chinese, and then we can pick up your money on the way back, sailor."

The man of the sea looked at him, teeth bared through his beard in a cunning grin. "And then slit my gullet after you've found my coin? Oh, no, matey. You'll have to do better than that. That coin is Sailor Morton's. You send your men for the heathens. Just tell Garcia to bring them to Jim Cort's camp. I'll stay here and rest up a few days."

"You'll go with us," the raider said, and it was final. He turned to Smith. "Get your boys rolling and hit for the Gulf, whatever men you think you'll need. Pick up them Chinese—one hunred dollars a head, cash in advance—and take them up the *Concepcion* to Cort's camp. Get some man of Valesquez's to guide you. Make Garcia do it, if necessary. We'll be waiting for you in Cort's hidden

46

camp. He's on his way to Tucson to sell some jewels and won't be back for a while. Savvy?"

"Yep," Smith answered. "All clear. But why couldn't we bring 'em across from the Gulf?"

"Because you might get picked up by patrols. They're thicker over that way. And because we're going to raid Jim Cort's camp and pick up his cache of money. Pancho ought to be able to find it. It'll pay fer that one man we lost and that burn you got across the hip. Get going," he finished.

An hour later Smith and five picked men rode out of camp, heading across the desert. They had a string of nine pack mules, loaded down with provisions. No mounts for the sixty Chinese. They would pay one hundred dollars apiece to get into Arizona—and walk every foot across the desert.

Sailor Morton drank more of the whiskey and went to sleep in a spare bunk in Lon Pearson's cabin. The afternoon wore on and night fell. Men ambled through the darkness from one cabin to another, talking and chatting. Their dark-eyed women sat in little groups and talked in Spanish. From somewhere in the distance came the bleat of a milk goat. The night wore on, and Sailor Morton, unused to riding, slept.

The camp came alive just before daybreak. Morton came out of his bunk, stiff-legged and swearing. He and Pearson ate a breakfast of flapjacks and salt pork and eggs from the chicken pens of one of the Mexican women, and saddled horses appeared out of nowhere.

The sailor swung up. The saddle with its stirrups felt much better. He was still thinking of his gold, and cursing the bad luck that had lost him Jim Cort's stolen pack train.

They got under way shortly before sunup—five men: Pearson, Sailor Morton, and three of Pearson's raiders leading pack mules loaded down with water and provisions for a long ride across the desert.

The sailor's muscles had limbered up a bit by now; but he was still thinking of his gold, and he didn't trust Pearson. The raider seemed to read his thoughts as they rode side by side.

"If you're worrying about that money, then forget it," he finally observed. "I play fair and square with my men. You're one of them, if you want to join. Nobody steals from anybody else in this outfit."

"Fair enough, matey," the sailor said. "I'm your man."

They rode on, came to the place where the seaman had lost the pack train to the Army officer, passed it and went on. Morton pointed ahead.

"Up there in them canyons is where the fracas started," he said. "Them sojers hit the Indians and I got away with the pack train while they was fightin' and shootin'. I hid my gold up there under some rocks."

"No use in packing it all the way south and then back again," Pearson said. "We'll pick it up on the return trip. Let's go over and see what kind of a fight they had."

They swung over to where the Apaches had been eating the shot down cow. It still lay there, partly skinned, with big chunks of meat cut out of its hips and back. The blow flies were at it, and the carcass was odorous, starting to swell.

"There's one of 'em," Pearson said, and pointed. They rode over.

The Apache had been shot squarely through the backbone and lay where he had fallen. The men began to circle. They found five more bodies.

"Twelve or thirteen, you said," Pearson speculated. "That means the soldiers got about half of them before the others got clear. Maybe they went south. If they did, we might run into 'em. Look around, boys, scatter out and follow tracks."

Presently a man came loping back. He hauled up beside where Pearson and Morton lounged in their saddles.

"They swung north—about six of 'em," he said. "Headin' like bats out of Hades back to the reservation. We follered the tracks of their horses—the ones who didn't git away. From the tracks it looks like the soldiers caught their hosses an' took 'em back to the fort."

"All right," the raider said. "Get the boys together and we'll go on."

They got under way and within a few minutes came to the place where the pack train had stopped. Morton hauled up and went down the slope on foot. Pearson heard a roar of frustrated rage and looked up to see his new man coming back.

"Gone!" Sailor Morton was bellowing, waving his huge arms. "My money's gone. Maybe Cort—maybe the sojers —maybe them bloody Indian pirates, I don't know. But my gold is gone!"

Chapter Seven

RED BARTON, the stage driver on the Tucson-to-Tombstone run, collected his pay in the Wells-Fargo office that afternoon about two and tucked the gold coins and silver into a pocket with a grin. He was a man forty years old, squat and powerful, and devoted to his wife and three children. It was a ritual with him that on pay day he would stop off and buy a present for his wife and what he called *muchachos*. His three boys. He took off his hat

49

and scratched with a horny hand at his thick shock of flaming hair.

"You know, of course," the clerk said, "that you'll be making the Tombstone run in the mornin'?"

"Heck, I ought to," Red grinned. "With all them gamblers an' sportin' women and the rest of 'em loadin' down the old hack every trip in to get rich in thet camp. Near wears my teams out in this hot weather. Ast the boss when he's goin' to git me some decent hosses." And Red grinned again.

"*You* ask him!" retorted the clerk. "I like this job and I ain't aiming to be fired off it. We got the best hosses in the country and you know it."

"What've we got lined up for the mawnin'?"

The clerk picked up a sheet of paper. "Let's see. You got one gent who looks like an Eastern drummer, going to Fairbanks. Then you got three more—some important-looking Easterner, his wife, and their daughter, down to Vail. Name's Anderson."

"Easterners!" snorted Red disgustedly. "All I haul is Easterners any more. They groan an' they grouch about the heat, the dust, the grub at the relay stations, an' one dam' fool swore a mosquito bit him—in the middle of the day at a hundred and ten in the shade. I told the fool it was a horsefly. What'n the blue blazes is this bunch of doods stoppin' off in Vail fer? There ain't a hotel or roomin' house there. Nothin' but a store and one saloon."

"From what I hear, he's a big rich gent come West to retire. They're buying the Batton ranch down on the *Santa Cruz*. Batton is meeting them there to pick them up."

"Hah!" snorted Red. "A fee-nancier punchin' cows, chasin' Pearson's gang when they steal his hosses, an' not afraid of the Apaches off the reservation, eh? Hah!" he snorted again.

"Well, he paid for it," the clerk said.

Red left the office and went out through the compound.

Beneath the sheds were a half a dozen stage coaches, and one of them was having its wheels greased. That was the one he was taking out in the morning. Red went through the gate, turned into the street, and presently came into Johannes Bruckmann's big store. He ought to be able to find something special for his wife. The stage driver went into its cool, adobe interior and then hauled up short at the sight of Jim Cort. He went over and shook hands.

"Hello, Jim," he grinned. "Ain't seen you in a month of Sundays. How's it goin'? Just get in?"

"Last night," Cort said. "How's the stage business?"

"Same old grind," grunted Red. "Roll 'em along the road, bawl at 'em, bust 'em on the rumps with a whip, and watch out for road agents and Apaches. How long you stayin' with us?"

"Leaving in a few minutes," Cort replied.

"I'm goin' out on the Tombstone run in the mornin'," Red said. "Drop over that way sometime, Jim, and I'll buy you a drink."

"That's a promise," Cort smiled, and went out.

Red went back to make his purchases from Bruckmann —a big bearded man with a hook nose—and went on home.

He turned to the compound the following morning shortly before seven, carrying a canteen and a rifle. One of the hostlers already had the two wheelers in line and another was bringing up the two leaders at a trot. Red went inside, checked over the passenger list again, and the clerk slid over a piece of paper. Red signed for the strongbox and the mail sacks. He glanced over his passengers, the little man in the derby hat and the three others. The Andersons. He saw a big, important-looking man in his fifties, wearing a new broad-brimmed Stetson hat, a motherly-looking woman somewhat younger, and the prettiest girl he had ever laid eyes upon. He was used to pretty passengers, most of them dance hall girls. But this one had flaming red hair like his own, and the bluest eyes he had ever seen. He heard her say to the older man, "Father, I'm so excited I can hardly wait. Think of it. Living on a ranch where it's nice and quiet."

Her father smiled patronizingly. "That wouldn't, by coincidence, have anything to do with the fact that Captain Hardy is stationed at Fort Huachuca, would it, Redhead?"

"Father!" she exclaimed, and actually blushed.

The man in the derby came over importantly. "Driver, what time do we get to Fairbanks?" he demanded.

Red looked him over with a critical eye. "That's about a hundred and five to a hundred and ten miles, mister. We average about ten miles an hour—barrin' such things as holdups, Apache raiders, busted axles, loose tires, an' limpin' horses."

"Heavens!" exclaimed the other. "Holdups! Does it happen often?"

"Nope," Red said complacently. "Not often. It's been all of a week or ten days since Pearson an' his gang hauled me up a few miles outa Bensen an' got the drop on Ace there."

Ace's shadow had blocked the doorway in the early morning sun. He was a blank-faced man of about twenty-five. He wore criss-cross cartridge belts around his waist supporting two guns in holsters. He carried a double-barreled shotgun in one hand and a repeating rifle in the other.

"They're ready to roll, Red," he said, tonelessly.

"All right," Red said. He turned to the four passengers. "All right, folks. The baggage has been loaded an' lashed down an' we're all set. If you'll take yore seats, we'll get outa here."

He went over and hauled the strongbox to a shoulder, picking up the two small mail sacks beneath his other arm. Ace was already up in the driver's seat. He hauled up the strongbox and the sacks. A hostler stood holding the bridles of the leaders. Red went up over the hub, reached down and took the lines from the second hostler, and bent to peer down at his passengers.

"All set, folks?"

"All set," answered the voice of Neely Anderson.

"Turn 'em loose!" Red yelled and tightened the lines. The four hit the traces with a snap and the stage jerked forward.

The Tombstone run, across one hundred and twenty miles of desert, was under way.

In the coach Neely sat beside her mother as the town fell behind and the desert began. In the distance she soon made out the green belt of the *Santa Cruz* River—the river on which her new home was to be. Batton and her father had talked things over in Tucson, and now they were going out to look over the place and close the deal. She thought she was going to like it out there. Ever since Lee Hardy had come West, serving at various forts before being assigned to Huachuca, he had written her endless letters. On his last trip back east he had told her of the newly established fort, and asked her to marry him. She didn't know yet why she had asked him to wait a while longer until she could make up her mind. She thought of those early days, of people she had known, of James Van Cortland who also had wanted to marry her. She had wondered many times what had become of Jim. He had never written after that night she had laughed at him, jeered at him; called him a profligate. Looking back, she could see now how a remark like that could hurt a man, and how only a girl of eighteen would have done such a thing. Somewhere deep down inside of her was a tinge of regret over that action on her part. It had been an injustice, and she was frank enough to admit it to herself. She knew only that he was somewhere out west here in this country. Captain Hardy's last letter had mentioned that fact: that Jim was a desperado, a gun fighter, a smuggler. He had turned mean and hard.

53

She reached into her bag and pulled out his last letter, reading it again as the stage rocked on. It had been posted to her in Tucson two weeks before.

"Don't tell me you're reading that letter again—that one from Bertie?" her mother asked.

"There's nothing else to do," Neely laughed. "And, Mother. you mustn't call him Bertie any more. He asked you not to. He's Captain Hardy now."

"He might be Captain Hardy to the others, but he'll be Bertie to me even if he becomes a major or a general or something."

"He's expecting to be promoted to major," she said. "But I'm astounded that he ran into Jim Cort out here."

"Jim Cort," sniffed her mother. "A young man from one of the best of families who couldn't live up to tradition. A hard drinker and a waster who threw away a good career in the Army. And now no better than a common stage robber."

Neely had read parts of the letter to her parents.

She put the letter away again, and the stage rolled on. They made the first way station in an hour and thirty minutes, covering fifteen miles. Red climbed down from his seat and handed the lines of the four sweaty horses to a hostler. He came over and opened the door of the coach.

"We'll be here about ten minutes, folks," he said. "Better go inside and stretch yore legs. We'll be rolling again as soon as we git a fresh change of hosses."

They got out and crossed over to a porch with its welcoming shade. A young Mexican woman came to meet them—wife of one of the hostlers. "Welcome," she said in fairly good English. "The rooms for you are out there, señoras. I have the coffee and beer and water for you to drink."

Presently Neely came back onto the porch. The heavily armed Ace stood beside the doorway, smoking a cigarette. Neely went up to him.

54

"How long have you lived out here, guard?" she asked.

"All my life, ma'am," he said.

"I guess you know a lot of people."

"Tol'able."

"Did you ever hear of a man named Captain Hardy, at the fort?"

"Seems like I heard the name, ma'am."

He was aloof, cool, indifferent. This was old stuff to him.

"What about this man named Jim Cort?" she asked, trying to make it sound casual.

"I've heard of him," was the reply.

Red had come onto the porch. The hostlers were jumping another four horses into place in front of the stage and working over trace chains. She turned to Red.

"Have you ever seen this Cort?" she asked.

Red was rolling a cigarette, getting in a few last puffs before they got under way again. He licked the brown paper and stuck it in a corner of his mouth.

"Just heard of him, ma'am," he said.

It was a rebuff and she knew it. These Westerners were a strange breed. She'd heard that you weren't supposed to ask questions. "You folks better git loaded," Red said.

They climbed back inside and took their seats while Red checked his wheels and the axles. He went up over the right hub and Neely heard him yell at the four horses. The coach jerked forward and the station disappeared in the dust behind. The sun rose higher and it grew hotter. More dust than wind came in through the open windows, and Neely saw the look of discomfiture and disgust on the drummer's face and smiled. He had tried to make conversation with her but had soon given it up as a bad job. She wasn't interested. Her thoughts were, for some strange reason, wrapped up in two men, and she had the equally strange premonition that she would see both of them within another month.

It was while she was looking out across a nearby arroyo that she saw the head with a red tag around it appear back of a raised rifle. The gun crashed in the Apache's hand and a scream broke from Mrs. Anderson as Ace's body tumbled past the window.

The stage leaped forward like a thing alive, Red's roar to the horses coming with the slashing pops of his whip. "Git!" he was bellowing. "Git outa here. Run, you sons of———like you never run before!"

"Neely!" screamed Mrs. Anderson. "Get your head back inside. You'll be shot!"

"I want to see it before I do," she shouted back.

The stage was shooting along the flat road, the horses at a dead run. Back of it she saw seven wild, fierce-looking men digging moccasined heels into the sides of their ponies. Fear chilled her to the marrow as she saw the ochre paint streaks below their cruel eyes. The dark faces were triumphant. They were shooting now, but apparently not at the stage. They were shooting at Red. Two of the bucks, better mounted than the others, had swung out on each side and were gradually drawing up abreast. Red was holding the lines in one hand now, firing his pistol with the other. He crippled the horse on his right, but the rider on his left had come up to the fore, and was closing in closer to the lumbering stage for a better shot, knowing Red couldn't reload his pistol. His high-pitched yell of triumph sent panic into the passengers.

Then Neely Anderson saw a sight that would forever live in her memory: a rider astride a long-legged, desert-bred horse came up out of an arroyo leading a pack mule. He dropped the rope and the horse shot forward. The rider bent down, swooping back up again with a repeating Winchester in his hand. He came in at a dead run, the horse's belly low above the ground, slashing a path through the greasewoods, straight at the hard-spurring Apache closing in toward the left front wheelers where Red cursed as he frantically tried to use his Winchester with one hand.

Never had she seen such a magnificent figure of man and horse as that hard-running gelding who came barreling toward them with bushy mane flying, and the lean figure of the rider holding the reins across its neck, a rifle in his hand.

He was thirty yards away when Neely recognized him and a strange cry broke from her. It was then, at her cry of "Jim Cort. *Oh, Jim, Jim, Jim!*" that the Apache saw him. The buck tried to swerve, to throw up his gun, and their horses almost collided as Cort swung the barrel of the repeater. It caught the Indian just in back of his head and crushed his skull.

Cort hit the ground and was down on one knee in a flash. The repeater went up and began to crash. Bullets from riders on running horses fifty yards away threw up dirt spurts all around him. They broke to circle him, and never completed the circle because Jim Cort killed five of them with five shots. The riderless horses went loping away into the greasewood, and Cort rose. The stage had swung around and Red was loping them back. He hauled up in a cloud of dust and grinned pantingly.

"Jim," he panted. "I'll buy you *two* drinks next time I see you in Tombstone."

But Cort didn't see or hear. He stood frozen, something hard gripping him inside, as he found himself looking straight into the eyes of Neely Anderson.

Chapter Eight

JIM REMOVED his hat as Neely and the others got out of the coach, and she saw a face that was the same as of old and yet different; an older face that had been burned to a light bronze by years beneath desert suns. She saw brittle eyes with no emotion in them, the heavy pistol at his hip, the big rifle in his left hand.

"Why, if it isn't James Van Cortland!" gasped out Mrs. Anderson with a sharp intake of breath. "Jimmie! After all these years."

Red sat on the box, staring. He removed his hat, scratched with one finger, put it back on.

Cort said, "How are you, Mrs. Anderson? Mr. Anderson, glad to see you again, sir. You're looking well, Neely."

That was all; cold and blank, the words without emotion. It was as though the years along the border had dried all feeling from his body.

Anderson shook hands eagerly. Mrs. Anderson preened herself. Neely came forward and extended a slim hand. "Jim, I don't know what to say. These Apaches—"

"Driver," called the excited drummer, "I'd like to go out and look at one of those Indians this man killed."

"Mister, we got another man down the road about a quarter or half-mile who ain't an Indian we got to look at," came the reply. "Get back in. They got Ace, Jim. Shot

58

him off the box from an arroyo. Don't know whether he's dead or not. Wish you'd lope down and see while I bring the stage on. Get in, folks. Hurry it up."

They got in and Cort went loping ahead. He found the body of Ace beside the road and swung down. One look at the shotgun guard told him that Ace had ridden his last ride. He had been shot through and through with a 45-70 Springfield, the owner of the gun having taken it from the fort when he had finished his tenure of one year as an Apache policeman. A feeling of regret went through Cort. He had liked Ace. Cort got his mail in care of Red, in Tucson, and it had been Ace who had climbed down between Vail and Benson, and disappeared into an arroyo to leave letters beneath a big flat rock. They had laughingly referred to it as Cort's "rural mail box."

The stage hauled up beside him and Red set the brake and climbed down. Neely got out again, followed by the others. She stifled a shudder as she looked down at the dead man.

Cort said, "He's dead, Red. The ball went clean through and tore a big hole. Looks like a 45-70."

"Probably one of those Apache police with a stolen Army gun," Red said savagely. "I'd like to kill every one of the—" And he finished a word that made the women's ears burn. "We've made eighty-three runs together between Tucson and Tombstone, and there never was a better shotgun guard—even if Lon Pearson's gang did git the drop on him once. Damn it to hell!" And he swore again. "He always liked you, Jim."

Neely Anderson stood there, listening to it all and stifling her shudders. She understood now that blank, hard emotionless expression on Jim Cort's face. So this was what the raw, wild border country could do to a man. It had seemed only minutes ago that she had asked the dead guard if he knew Jim Cort. And he had said, quietly and

59

with that certain aloofness in his voice, "I've heard of him."

"I always liked Ace, too," Cort said, and put on his hat. He looked at the driver. "Well, Red, I guess I'd better go out and round up those Apache horses and try to return them to their rightful owners."

"All right, Jim. I'll take the tarp off the baggage and lash him on top and take him on into Tombstone. He's got some folks somewhere round here. I'll try to git in touch with 'em."

Cort mounted again, and as he rode off Neely saw that he was shoving fresh shells into the magazine of the rifle before returning it to its saddle scabbard. Red went up on top of the coach and unloosed the tarp, tossing it down. He rolled Ace's body into it and, aided by the two other men, lifted it to the top, where he lashed it down. They drove back to the place where Cort had killed the five Apaches and went out to look. Neely saw dead men for the first time: wild, savage-looking men with dark faces, with lateral streaks of paint beneath the eyes and across their noses. Faces fierce even in death. Cort came back, leading his own pack animal and six horses that had belonged to the raiders. He removed the blanket saddles and tossed them aside while the others stood looking down at the body of a large, well built buck. Cort swung down.

"That's Deer Tail," Cort said to Red. "He was a minor chief and friend of Geronimo. They broke off the reservation a couple of weeks ago, him and about a dozen others, on a raiding spree south and heading for Mexico to join Geronimo."

"He in Mexico now?" Red asked.

Cort nodded. "I saw him down there several days ago. He said he was willing to have a talk with the soldiers, if they'd give him a square deal and listen to his complaints. Anyhow, Deer Tail hit south, and ran into a patrol of Hardy's men while they—the Indians—were eating a shot

60

down cow. Hardy and his men got about half of them and the others headed north again, supposedly for the reservation. But they've been raiding and stealing horses, and raising general ructions, before they went back. That crack at the stage probably was a final spree before they burned the breeze back, all innocence."

"Well," Red grunted in satisfaction, "they won't be raidin' off the reservation no more—not this bunch." Then he turned as a sound came from behind. "Well, I'll be jiggered! Here come the cavalry—late as usual."

There were about a dozen of them, and Cort stood stony-faced as he recognized Hardy. One of the troopers led two pack mules. They were dusty, tired-looking, their mounts sweaty. Neely Anderson gave a sudden cry.

"Mother! Father! Look, it's Bert."

It was Hardy, all right, and the first thing Cort noticed was that he wore the insignia of a major on his dusty blue shoulders.

Hardy had led his captured pack train back to the scene of the fight, and waited until his men had come straggling in, after the running fight. The success of the patrol had exceeded his wildest imagination. They had been out two days and got a rich pack train and killed several Apache raiders. He had curbed his impatience to get back to the fort and report to the "Old Man," and the result had fulfilled his expectations. The general had come in, and Hardy had been promoted to the permanent rank of a major on the spot. They had wanted him to take over an administration job, at a desk, but this he had skillfully declined. He wanted to be in the field, to make combat reports, to get quicker promotion so that he might wear those coveted eagles on his shoulders, and to see Neely. For his now daily letters to her in Tucson, sent by military post mail to and from Tucson each day, had brought the information that they were buying the Batton ranch. It would be easy, in the field, to drop by that ranch at regular intervals, sometimes to "rest" up his men overnight while he spent his time with her and the family.

The new Major Hardy had asked for, and received, permission to hit out again with a compact dozen men to run down those remaining raiders or drive them back to the reservation. He had been hot on their trail when he and his men topped the ridge and saw the motionless stagecoach.

Hardy rode up. The first person he saw was Neely, and then Jim Cort, and a dead Indian. He didn't know why, but something told him that Cort had killed that Indian. That meant a raid on the coach, and Hardy felt a knot in his stomach.

He pulled up, still the stern disciplinarian, and his gauntleted hand went up in salute to Neely and her folks before he swung down.

He went to Neely first, and without hesitation swept her into his strong arms and kissed her. It was a bold thing to do; bolder than he would ever have tried under other circumstances. But Cort was there. Hardy felt the weight of the new oak leaves on his shoulders, and the gesture was a possessive one.

"Bert!" she gasped out, freeing herself. "Bert—I—where did you come from?"

"We were trailing those raiders," he said. "We'd have got them in a few hours." This for her benefit. He knew he had arrived too late.

He was shaking hands with her parents, his hat off. Cort stood by the horses, calmly smoking a cigarette. His eyes said nothing. Neely thought she caught a look of contempt in them. Red had instinctively gone back up over a wheel and was in the driver's seat.

Hardy looked at Cort. He was all officer now, aware of Neely's presence. "You kill these Indians?" he asked curtly.

"Yes," Cort said.

"You can consider yourself under military arrest pending an investigation as to the murder of Apaches technically at peace and wards of the United States Government."

"I notice you said *you* were chasing them," Cort said.

"That's a military job, not covered by civil regulations," was the curt reply. "That's our job."

"You didn't seem to be doing to good at it when they killed the stage driver's shotgun guard off the coach and attacked it," Cort sneered.

"That matter will be taken care of through channels. Men, take that smuggler into custody," Major Hardy ordered.

From atop the stage came the peculiar mechanical sound of a rifle cartridge being jacked fast into the firing chamber. Red sat there, not covering Hardy, the repeater merely being pointed downward. The troopers saw it, and hid secret grins. They made no move in the face of Hardy's orders. This was something he'd have to handle himself.

"Arrest him!" Hardy snapped out to his men.

"I don't think, Mister Hardy," came Red's voice, "that they'd better try it."

"Why?"

"Because the moment they try it I'm going to blow the top of yore head off with this first shot and then see how many more I can pump outa the magazine of this repeater before they git me."

"Hold it, Red!" came Cort's sharp voice. "I'll do the shooting if they make the try." And to Hardy: "Just go ahead and give the order again. Bert. When you do, you're a dead man. They'll get me, but I'll get you first."

"You're resisting military arrest?" Hardy said coldly.

"Go ahead and try it and see what happens," came the hard reply.

Neely Anderson stood beside her mother, a hand unconsciously holding the older woman's arm. She saw Cort's right hand lying close to the heavy pistol at his right hip,

63

the repeater across Red's lap up in the driver's seat, the hidden grins on the faces of the troopers. She saw indecision come into Major Hardy's face; he who had written her such passionate love letters, asking her to become Mrs. Hardy. Hard, atavistic men all, in a hard, wild desert country. Cort had just killed and now he was ready to kill again.

She looked at Hardy once more.

He looked at Cort, and a cold shrug moved his square shoulders. He had written to Neely, telling her of the killing of the Apaches and the capture of the smuggler pack train. He had even held out two bolts of the silk to give her at the ranch. But Hardy saw the repeater in the hands of the grinning stage driver, the dead Indian on the ground; and he saw Jim Cort's right hand hanging close by the big pistol at his hip. He knew when the odds were against him. His own men were secretly pleased. He could sense it.

"All right, Jim," he said casually. "It would have been a mere technicality anyhow. We'll call it off because that man on the stage is just fool enough to shoot. I'll see you later, mister," he added.

"Mister," Red grinned back, "don't try it while I'm drivin' this stage. The Wells-Fargo people have a powerful lot of influence, and the Post Office department of Uncle Sam is plumb sensitive about people who stop stages with mail sacks on 'em. You ever try stoppin' this stage, and they'll bust you back to a mule-tendin' buck private, where you belong."

Hardy had to recover face somehow. He turned to his men. "All right, boys, get a burying detail to work and dig some graves for these Indians. You, Sergeant Toland, take charge of those six horses."

Cort's voice said coldly. "Four of them, Bert. All wearing Batton's brand. The other two are unbranded. They're mine."

"We'll take the six."

"Here we go again." Red grinned like a gargoyle. "You

might be knowin' all about military law, mister, but you ain't up to date on the rest of it. Them two unbranded hosses belong to Jim. Take it, or the United States Cavalry and Wells-Fargo are goin' to go six hands 'round."

Chapter Nine

CORT TURNED his back and walked off toward the horses. It was a gesture of contempt toward Major Hardy. He knew that the officer had kissed her for Cort's benefit. It wouldn't have been in his nature to do otherwise, in front of his men and her parents.

Cort picked up the lead ropes on his pack animal and the two unbranded horses. He rode off without a word or a backward glance, neither seeing nor knowing of the disappointment in Neely Anderson's eyes.

Her father cleared his throat to cover his general embarrassment. He took off the new western hat and mopped at his forehead. "Whew!" he said in relief. "What a day it has been. I'm becoming a bit dubious about buying this Batton ranch, Cap—er, Major Hardy. At any rate, it doesn't appear as though things will prove dull."

"If you mean the Indians, we've got the fight pretty well whipped out of them except for sporadic raids such as this one. And we can take care of the ones from Sonora without too much trouble. Neely wrote me you'd be on today's stage to Vail, and I was worried when we were hot on their trail in this direction. I think we'd better accompany you to the ranch. We'll probably catch up with you somewhere south of Vail."

The burying detail already were hard at work with shovels, scooping out shallow graves in the soft sand. Red loaded up his passengers and got ready to go on. Hardy came over and bent from the saddle to look into the coach; square-shouldered and every inch the leader. "We'll see you at the ranch tonight," he said. "Goodbye now."

Red yelled at his team and the coach sped off at a trotting pace. Neely looked back. Then she looked out the other side to where, in the distance, the lone figure of a horseman moved southward through the greasewood, leading three other animals. He topped a ridge, and then she saw him disappear from sight in an arroyo.

She settled back in the seat and remained silent, her thoughts turbulent and upsetting. Sight of Cort had struck fire in her, and she wondered if it was because he'd put in an appearance at a time when his help was needed. Or was it bcause she had seen in his grim, desert-burned face the knowledge that as far as he was concerned, there wasn't any past? He had put it all behind him, buried it deep in six years as a rider of the desert wastes.

Her father glanced over at her. "Getting tired, Redhead?" he asked fondly, smiling a little quizzically.

"A little," she said.

They rolled into Vail in another hour or so and Red hauled up before two buildings: a false-fronted general store and a false-fronted saloon. The girl saw a few riders lounging about; quiet-looking fellows who eyed her indifferently but with looks that told of hunger for the sight of a beautiful woman. Red jumped down and the passengers got out.

A man with an exceptionally dirty white apron around his waist came out of the saloon and looked at the driver.

" 'Lo, Red," he greeted him. "Yo're a little late. Gittin' old, or somethin'?"

66

"No," Red grunted. "Just scared. 'Paches hit us a way back; part of that bunch the soldiers got a little while back."

The indolence went out of the idling men's bodies. They came erect.

"The devil you say!" gasped out the barkeep.

"Ho, Red," boomed a big voice, and another man came through. This was Batton, the Santa Cruz rancher; big, bluff, hearty-looking. "What's this about the redskins?"

Red told him. "They got Ace," he said. "He's up there in a tarp. But Jim Cort busted up the show. How about some of you fellers giving me a hand lifting him into the seat while I unload these folks' baggage?"

The Andersons were greeting Batton and the two men shook hands. Neely noticed for the first time the big hack with four horses by the side of the building. It had a Circle B branded on one side, Batton's brand. A motherly-looking woman who could have been only the rancher's wife came from the store, her arms filled with packages. Neely and her mother walked over to the hack with her.

"Land sakes alive," she said, stowing them beneath the back seat, on the floor. She turned wiping sweat from her face. "I thought the cavalry had those pesky devils pretty well tamed, but just about every time we think so they break out again, seems like. But it's sure a lot better than it was ten-fifteen years ago, before we didn't have any fort and few soldiers. They gave us a time of it, I can tell you. So Cort happened to come by? Maybe he's got a bad reputation among some folks for some things, but there never was more of a gentleman. And they killed Ace? What a terrible shame! His folks lived not more'n thirty miles from us. He was only twenty-four and I've known him since he was a little tyke."

Red was handing down baggage to willing hands and Mrs. Batton went over as the last piece came down. She looked up at the puffing, red-faced driver.

67

"What are you going to do with Ace's body, Red?" she asked.

"Take him on into Tombstone an' plant him, Miz Batton. He won't keep long in this hot weather. I got to get word to his folks. Seems like he said they're over here in this part of the country, som'eres."

"You take him on into the undertaking parlor and tell 'em to hold him as long as possible. I'll get word to them. Don't know how his mother is goin' to take it, poor soul." She turned to one of the riders. "LeRoy, you get on that horse of yourn and go tell Ace's folks. It's near fifty miles but you can get fresh horses at Haines' and the Double Arroyo ranches. You lay over there and help around the place while they're gone. Tell her I wish we could come, but we got visitors and the ranch to look after."

A swivel-hipped young puncher said, "All right, Miz Batton. Soon's I git my canteen filled I'll git goin'."

Batton and another of his riders were helping each other lash the baggage into the hack, and still leave room for the five people. Neely saw the young puncher come out of the saloon with a dripping canteen in one hand. He went to a horse bearing the Circle B brand, tied on the one-gallon metal canteen, and swung up.

"Be back in a few days," he said briefly to Batton, and jogged off around the corner, heading south and east into the desert wastes.

Neely stood there and watched him go, riding fifty miles across the desert in an effort to aid "a neighbor." And it came to her then, the full impact of if, just how big this country was—it and its people. A stagecoach guard had been killed by attacking Apaches, there had been a fight in which more men died, and seemingly within minutes life was flowing on again the same as usual.

She remembered something she had heard Batton say in Tucson: "This desert can be good to the strong an' bad to the weak. You either whup it or it whups you. There ain't any middle course out here." And she knew that day in Vail that she was facing a hard task in adjusting herself to this new way of life.

Batton's other cowhand took the hack and drove over to water the horses and fill the canteens. He came back and the five got in, the two men up front. The three women took the rear seat. They got under way, taking a "road" that was more of a trail, heading in a southerly direction. Mrs. Batton reached down from somewhere and pulled out a big basket covered with white cloth.

"I had an idea you folks would be hungry, so I brought along lunch. The chicken is probably pretty cold—I cooked it at three o'clock this morning before we left the ranch—but you can make out until we get home."

They drove all that afternoon, and now men appeared out of the desert—men in blue. Hardy rode in close and exchanged greetings and the cavalry patrol accompanied them. Neely looked at the four led horses.

"Heck, them looks like some of my hosses, Anderson!" the rancher suddenly exclaimed. "Why, shore—I'd know thet long-legged claybank anywhere. The red devils stole him an' several more two-three nights ago, and left some played out hosses they'd stole from Haines."

"Those are the four I was telling you about," Anderson said. "Cort took the other two, the unbranded ones."

"Wal, if they belong to any of us ranchers along the Santa Cruz betwixt here and where Lon Pearson and his raiders hole up, they'll be turned back to their right owners."

"So you know Cort?" Neely heard her father ask in surprise.

"Know him? Shore, I know him, Anderson. He stops by our place every now and then. Strange man."

"I've heard something about him,." Neely's father commented cautiously.

"I expect you hev. Any man who plays a lone hand like

69

Jim does is bound to be talked about. Shore, I know—he's supposed to be a smuggler, a gun fighter, an' maybe even a' outlaw. But out here we take a man fer what he's worth, an' not what he does, *thet* part of it bein' his own business. You seen what happened today. If Jim hadn't come along, yore wife would be dead by now an' your daughter on the back of a' Apache hoss. You didn't see me in Wilcox with a tough bunch of cattle on my han's an' waitin' four days for cattle cars while my wife was took down sick . . . an' Jim Cort standin' by after he near killed a horse ridin' sixty miles for a doctor."

He grunted, and that grunt said that they'd better not talk about it any more.

They left the desert late that afternoon, dropping down into flatter river-bottom land that was green. In the distance the line of cottonwood trees cut a verdant swath through the brownness, the desolation that surrounded them. The soldiers rode off to one side, dusty and tired. Neely herself had never realized that anybody could be as tired or as hungry as she was. The heavily loaded hack reached the river, and Batton pulled them up in four inches of water to let them suck away thirstily, with heads lowered. Two miles away lay ranch buildings.

"There she is," Batton boomed out, pointing with his buggy whip.

The hack ground on across. The wheels sank deep into dry, powdery sand as they went on at a walk. They came out onto harder ground and drove in among cottonwood trees, and all of a sudden it was delightfully cool.

"Notice the difference?" Mrs. Batton asked. "That's the desert. Hot during the day, cool in the evenings. The cottonwoods draw moisture."

They drove on among the cottonwoods for another mile, pulled up to higher ground, and came into a lane between fences of barbed wire. It was hard packed, and on either side lay green fields of alfalfa. Neely saw men in the fields,

70

working with shovels. Water poured out of well constructed irrigation ditches.

"I irrigate," Batton explained. "I bought a steam engine an' a big pump from a mine outfit that went busted an' sunk a big well just above the ranch buildings over there. We only had to go thirty feet to git all the water we need, an' it'll handle a four-inch flow. I raise the alfalfa for my blooded hosses an' some milk cows an' work teams. The cattle forage for themselves. Only trouble we have is thet they keep breakin' down fences to git at the alfalfa. Then they eat, git bloated, an' lay down an' die——unless we can sometimes save 'em by stickin' a knife between their ribs an' lettin' the gas off their stomachs."

Neely said, her eyes glistening at sight of the sprawling adobe buildings, "It's beautiful. I've never seen anything like it."

"You should have seen it when Pa and me first came out here." Mrs. Batton smiled. "I handled a scraper and team right alongside him to level that land for irrigation. We built the first room of our house with four portholes in it, so's we could see four different directions every morning before we opened the door. Them Apaches was mean in them days."

The hack rattled by a Mexican on a burro, herding a group of goats down the lane. Mrs. Batton explained:

"We have about a dozen Mexicans here with their families, who work the fields. They like goat milk. Our regular riders handle the cattle. Pa, how many riders have we got now?"

Batton's answer was a question. He turned in the seat as they neared the buildings.

"Who's thet man just rode up in front of the house? Looks like Lon Pearson."

Mrs. Batton peered out. "It is, Pa. Now what do you suppose that outlaw wants with us?"

Nobody replied. Neely's eyes were on the man as they

71

rolled up to a stop in front of the low, rambling adobe house with the big porch across the east side. She was suddenly very glad that Hardy and his men were clattering up the lane in back of them.

Chapter Ten

THEY RODE up and pulled to a stop, Neely getting out wearily. She paid no attention to the bold look of the handsome man on the horse. Her folks followed her down. Batton had got to the ground, handing the lines to a Mexican youth. The soldiers were clattering up.

Batton looked up at Pearson a little belligerently.

"What're you doin' here, Lon?" he asked bluntly.

Pearson didn't answer for a moment. After leaving the place where Sailor Morton had lost his gold he and his men had ridden on southward, out of the *Oro Blancos* and into the desert. The trail to Cort's camp was easy to follow now, the tracks deep in the soft surface that was mostly sand. They crossed the line and drove on, and it was about sundown when they reached Cort's camp. Sailor Morton swung down with a grunt of relief. He was stiff and sore, not being used to riding.

"Yep, this looks like it, all right," the raider said with satisfaction. "Now to keep a sharp lookout fer Apaches and find Cort's cache while we wait fer Smitty to bring them Chinese up the river."

They made camp, ate a big supper, and slept with

Pancho on guard. Nothing happened. Early the next morning they were up and, after breakfast, Pearson turned to the half Apache-half Mexican and grinned expectantly.

"All right, you danged 'breed. Show some of that Apache blood. Find Cort's cache."

Pancho was short and squat because of his mother's blood, but he was a tower of strength and endurance. He put on moccasins and began to circle the camp. Pearson and the others waited.

"Don't forget," Sailor Morton warned. "If that blasted Indian of Cort's grabbed my gold and brought it back here, there ain't going to be any split on it, matey. I'd have settled Cort's hash later anyhow."

They waited for half an hour. Then from somewhere over the ridge they heard a call. Lon Pearson rose and tossed away his cigarette. "Come on boys. Pancho's found tracks."

They climbed up among the rocks and topped the ridge. Down below the half-breed stood gesticulating. The party went down and came up beside the trailer.

"Here his tracks," he said in bad English. "You come."

He set off and they followed him. Cort had stepped on rocks whenever possible, but a smudge of dirt here and an unusual spot of color there were the same as a boardwalk to the trailer's black eyes. They dropped further down, worked along the floor of the gulley, and the 'breed turned into the yawning jaws of a canyon. Here the trail ended abruptly.

Pancho went up among the rocks, jumping from one to the other like a small lizard, his black eyes darting. He circled, came down to the floor of the canyon, went up the other side. The men below waited and smoked.

Then there came a sharp cry from the 'breed and he pointed to a boulder. Pearson and his men began an eager scramble. They climbed up, and by the time they got to the place Pancho had the boulder rolled aside. There was

73

a big hole hollowed out beneath it and the hole was empty —all except a scrap of white paper. The raider snatched it up and read the writing.

Pearson: When Sailor Morton set off with my pack train of silk, I merely picked up his gold to pay for the contraband and the mules. A fair swap. But I had a hunch that if he followed the river he'd run into your outfit. I figured you might come back to look for my cache. Well you've found it. Red Calf, my Apache helper, hid the Sailor's gold in another place, then came back here after my cache. Sorry to disappoint you boys. A long hot ride for nothing.
                                                    Jim Cort.

Lon Pearson tore the paper into bits and flung it aside while Sailor Morton, still stiff from the long miles astride two different mounts, swore savage oaths and vowed revenge. Valesquez had said this man Cort was a sharp one.

"A long ride fer nothing, eh?" gritted the raider. "He'll think different when we wait here in his camp and pick up them sixty Chinese. Blast his soul!"

Smitty had finally shown up at the camp, riding his horse along the bank with his men on each side of the river as guards for the flatboats loaded with Chinese. Pearson had made the deal with Garcia, taking over the sixty Chinese —who were not coolies but merchants and other men of money. Three or four of them spoke English with varying degrees of fluency. They were the leaders. Garcia finished the deal and went back down the river in the flatboats with the men of the ship. It had been an uneasy voyage for him, but no Apaches had attacked.

The Mexican had brought along big leather waterskins and these were filled that afternoon, after the Chinese had rested. At sundown the pack horses were loaded with rice and dried fish, plus supplies for the raiders, and in the moonlight a long line of plodding men began the trek northward toward the border. It was slow going because the aliens were not used to walking, and had been weeks and weeks aboard ship with little chance for exercise. Pearson studied them, set the pace at about two miles an hour, and then rested them for fifteen minutes.

At ten o'clock that night they camped in an arroyo in the desert, down below the lip of a bank. The moon was bright, a white ball in the sky, and you could see for an amazingly long distance. Small fires were struck along the sandy floor and the tired Chinese began cooking rice, while the outlaws kept guard upon the rim, eyes searching the night for Apaches.

It was said that Apaches didn't attack at night because the ghosts of their dead were abroad, roaming the land, and mustn't be disturbed. But Pearson had been on the border much too long to trust the red devils. He was taking no chances.

The chattering Chinese were eating hungrily when Pearson strolled up on the ridge to where the black-bearded "Smitty" sat with his back to a rock, smoking a cigarette, his horse nearby.

"Nice night," the raider chief observed, and sat down beside him.

"Yeah," Smitty said. "But them dam' fires down there make me nervous. I'll bet an Apache could see the glow for miles."

Pearson laughed, bringing out the makings. He rolled and lit. "You're getting nervous, Smitty. You can't make a living for that Mexican woman getting skittish. Anyhow, it takes a lot of fires to cook rice for the sixty slant-eyed heathen."

The bearded outlaw grunted and dropped his cigarette butt in the sand, covering it. "I know," he said. "But I'll sure feel a lot better when we get this bunch into Tucson an' turn 'em over to Bruckmann. Now thet's a sharp Dutchman. He lets us take all the risks an' he takes all the profits on anything thet's brought in. I shore don't know how he's goin' to handle as big a bunch as this in Tucson, but you can reckon thet thet Dutchman knows his business. Anyhow, I'll be plumb relieved when we get 'em in there."

"I was just thinking," the raider chief said casually, "that maybe we won't have to take 'em that far."

Smitty looked at him in surprise, his eyes narrowing in the moonlit night. "Yeah?"

"Seems to me they oughta be packin' a lot of coin on 'em. I was just wonderin', if we stripped 'em down, how much the haul would be."

"Thet thought has sorta been runnin' through my mind too."

Pearson rose. "We'll see," he said briefly, and left.

They let the Chinese finish eating and then sleep for two hours. The moon was far down toward the horizon when the outlaws woke up the tired aliens and got them under way once more. The long line of men in single file and in little groups plodded on, carrying their belongings, and the night grew colder. At daybreak the caravan finally came to a halt, making a dry camp. The outlaws cooked breakfast, but most of the exhausted Chinese flopped down and promptly went to sleep. Pearson put his men on guard, two of them at two-hour intervals, and rolled into his saddle blankets. The sun rose and grew hot. Men stirred, picked up their belongings, and sought what little shade the greasewoods had to offer. One of the Chinese, a big fat fellow who spoke broken English and could converse with Sailor Morton in a mixture of English and Chinese, appeared to be the leader. Pearson ordered him to make the others keep off the skyline, explaining about the Indians who might come at any moment, and the frightened Chinese communicated the warning to the others. Pearson went back to his saddle blanket beneath a huge yucca tree.

He woke up again in the afternoon and stretched lazily. The Chinese were cooking rice again and chattering among

76

the lane, followed by about a dozen cavalrymen. Sight of the uniforms caused some uneasiness in the mind of the raider. It was put aside at the sight of the woman who got out of the coach—the loveliest creature he had ever set eyes upon. Fire went through him at the sight of her. He saw the flaming red hair, the clear eyes, the lissome figure. He ignored the words of Batton. The rancher repeated them.

"What am I doing here?" Pearson smiled, swinging down. "Just want to talk a little business, Batton."

Chapter Eleven

HE CAME OVER and they shook hands, Batton a little reluctantly. Pearson's manner said that he wanted, and expected an introduction to Neely. Batton did the honors. Pearson removed his hat, and Neely had to admit that he was one of the handsomest men she had ever seen. He had manners, and his handclasp was gentle.

"The desert, Miss Anderson," he said gallantly, "has bloomed anew since you got here. I hope you like our country."

"Thank you," she murmured.

Hardy and his men had clattered up. The major swung down, and Batton turned to him.

"Of course you'll stay all night, Major," the rancher said.

"I believe we will, if it won't inconvenience you."

79

"Not at all. Not at all. We'll get some extra help in the kitchen an' rig up an extra table."

"That won't be necessary, sir. My men have their own supplies. They can camp down among the cottonwoods."

"All right. Let 'em rest up. They look ga'nted. But we've got an extra room in the house fer you."

"Thank you, sir," Major Hardy replied.

He gave his horse's reins to a soldier and issued crisp orders. He took a pack from back of his saddle and carried it inside as the troopers clattered off. They all came into a big living room, cool and comfortable-looking. Calfskin rugs were on the floor and the furniture was mostly of willow, covered with rawhide, and filled with homemade cushions. Neely thought she had never seen such a comfortable-looking place. She knew she was going to like this new home.

Batton had forgotten to introduce the officer and the outlaw. They shook hands a bit stiffly, but correctly and politely. Batton let out a bellow at a Mexican girl, and began talking rapid fire Spanish. He turned to Hardy.

"She'll show you where your room is, Major," he said. "You can clean up a bit if you like. We'll have supper in about an hour."

Batton didn't know what kind of "business" the raider wanted to talk over with him—since he was certain that some of his stolen horses had been taken by the raider and his men—but cow country courtesy demanded that he offer the hospitality of the ranch. Pearson was quick to accept. He put away his horse and prepared to stay overnight.

The ranch was a one-story affair with long wings running off east and west. A third wing comprised the kitchen and huge dining room. Neely Anderson found herself in a big room next to that of her parents. It was in the tip of the west wing. A flagstone veranda ran by the open window and she leaned there, looking out at the green fields, the

80

upward slope of the desert beyond, and listening to the chugging of the steam engine's big pump. Batton had rigged up a big wooden water tower down by one of the corrals and piped water into all the rooms. He had invented a crude solar heating system of tin barrels on the roof, and Neely gave a cry of delight at the sight of the long tin bathtub with its two spigots. Thumping sounds came from the hallway and a timid knock sounded on the door.

She opened it and saw two grinning Mexican youths with her trunks and suitcases.

"*Para usted, señorita,*" (for you, miss) one of them said, and they came in.

She used signs to show them where to put the baggage. "I'll have to learn Spanish, I'm afraid," she laughed.

They both grinned, and one said, "Is ver' izzy, *señorita.* W'en you wan' know somet'ing in esspanish, you say, '*Como se llama este en Español?*' It mean, 'How is that name in esspanish?' Ver' izzy."

She laughed in sheer delight, the weariness fleeing in an instant. She pointed to the bed. "*Como se llama este en Español?*" she asked.

"*Cama,*" was the grinning reply. "You learn ver' fast, I theenk."

They went out laughing, and she laughed too. She locked the door and laid out the clothes on the *cama,* and then removed her own, after pulling blinds over the windows. She revelled in the sleekness of her young body as she went in and began filling the long, handmade tin tub with very hot water. Had she known the water was heated by the sun she would have been astonished. She thought it came from the steam engine chugging away over by the well.

She bathed and put on the clean dress, and brushed her hair. The tiredness of the long ride across the desert had been replaced by a tingling excitement. She was having

81

dinner in her own new home tonight for the first time; Bert Hardy was in the house, and so was a bold-eyed man Mrs. Batton had said was an outlaw. They had been attacked by Apaches that very day—and out of a six-year-distant past had come Jim Van Cortland—out of the desert wastes on a running horse with a Winchester in his hands. He was somewhere out there this evening; alone, cold, implacable.

She had taken an hour to bathe, lying in the luxury of the big tub for long minutes before dressing, and now she heard a knock on the door. She opened it and saw Hardy. He held two big bundles in his arms.

Every spot of dust had been brushed from his blue uniform. His boots were newly shined and he was freshly shaven, his black moustache clipped carefully. She couldn't help comparing him with the bold, handsome, blond Lon Pearson—and with the lean, stony-faced Jim Cort.

"Hello, darling," he greeted her.

"Come in, Bert. What in the world do you have there?"

He placed the two bundles on the bed. "A little present for you, Neely. You wrote that you'd be on the stage today, coming to the ranch. So I brought these along, a rather scarce commodity in this country."

She opened the bundles, and a small cry of delight broke from her at sight of the two bolts of Chinese silk. One was snow white, the other a flaming red.

"Why, Bert!" she exclaimed breathlessly. "Bert—how in the world—where did you get them? They're lovely!"

"I captured one of Jim Cort's smuggler pack trains recently," he said casually. "Five pack mules loaded with these. Of course I had to turn the goods over to the fort commander, but the regulations do not say that I can't hold out two of them for the prettiest girl in the world, the future Mrs. Hardy."

"Why Bert, how thoughtful of you. I don't know what to say."

"Say it like this, Neely," he replied, and again she felt herself swept into his strong arms.

"Bert, you mustn't," she gasped out, freeing herself. "I—"

Then came the sound of a supper gong, ringing throughout the house.

They went out into the hallway and down it, and came into a huge dining room. There was a long table covered with a white tablecloth with plates and silver set out; enough to seat a dozen people. Mexican women were hurrying here and there with bowls filled with steaming dishes: roast beef, creamed potatoes, black-eyed peas, big pies and a peach cobbler. There were bowls of homemade "chow-chow," a green, spicy condiment. Pickled chili in jars, dried red peppers of the kind she had seen hanging in strips from a corner of the veranda, and two small bowls filled with what looked like green buckshot. She saw a huge jar of cool sweet milk and a steaming coffee pot set on a flat rock in the middle of the table.

The windows were open. It was now dusk. From the Alamo trees came the twitter of birds, and from somewhere in the distance came the bawl of a milk pen calf. The big steam engine had ceased its chugging. From off in the distance among the cabins inhabited by the Mexicans came the sounds of a woman's voice, singing, accompanied by a guitar. Her husband, playing for her as he waited for his supper, Neely Anderson thought.

People were filing into the room. Neely saw Lon Pearson, clean-shaven and with blond locks shining in the light of the lamps, enter. Batton was heading for the table. His wife was still directing the hurrying Mexican girls in staccato Spanish.

"Well, folks," boomed the rancher, "just grab a chair an' set down. Fust who gits to the table here in this house gits the most to eat."

They seated themselves. Batton sat at the head of the

table. Neely's parents sat at his left, Major Hardy and Neely at his right. Neely sat between Hardy and Lon Pearson. Mrs. Batton seated herself by Mrs. Anderson.

"Now, folks," the rancher said, "if you'll bow your heads, I'll say the blessing."

They bowed their heads.

"Oh Lord," Batton said over his plate, "we thank Thee for this food that has been placed before us. We ask you to forgive us any sins we might have committed this day, and look after us until the coming of a new dawn. Amen."

He raised his head. "Dive in, folks," he said.

It was then that Neely Anderson, raising her head from her plate, saw movement through the open door of the big living room beyond. A rider had come into view, leading a pack mule. He swung down and a cold hand clutched at her heart.

Batton had seen too. He rose from the head of the table. "Well, I'll be!" he exclaimed. "It's Jim Cort!"

Chapter Twelve

CORT PULLED UP, leading his pack animal. He saw the lights in the house but not those present in the dining room. The rancher shook hands eagerly.

"Howdy, Jim. Git down, man, git down. You're just in time for supper. I'll have one of the Mexicans take care of your horses. Say—I was up to Vail today an' heard plenty. Thanks for turnin' them hosses of mine over to Hardy."

"I noticed his men camped down among the cottonwoods. Maybe I'd better not stay overnight, Bat. I did want to talk business with you, but Hardy and I are not exactly friendly."

"You mean about thet pack train business he claims was yourn?"

"No," Cort said. "It was my train, all right, Bat, though it had been stolen by a man named Sailor Morton. I might as well tell you that I've known Hardy before now."

"I see," the rancher said thoughtfully. "I sorta got that impression from stories I heard about what happened between you and him at the stage this mornin'. Wal, you two can put it aside while you're here."

"I'd better go on and camp out. I can state my business right now. Bat, I'm through as a smuggler. Made my final deal with Bruckmann in Tucson this trip."

"Good, Jim. Want to go to work on this ranch? They'll need a good man around here."

"I want to buy this ranch from you, Bat. For cash," Jim Cort replied.

Batton whistled under his breath. "It's pourin' rain," he commented. "Because it just happens there happen to be some more people in the house with the same idee."

"Who?" Cort asked. "I'll outbid them, Bat."

"The Anderson family, who was on thet stage today when the 'Paches hit it, git first crack at it, Jim. We worked out most of the details in Tucson some time back. But just before sundown Lon Pearson showed up."

"Pearson?"

Batton grinned at the look of surprise on Cort's face. "Yep, rode up an' says as how he wants to buy this ranch. Nobody but Lon would do it, either—after stealin' my hosses the way he has."

"Why didn't you boot him off the ranch?" Cort demanded harshly.

That grin from the rancher again. "Because Anderson wants to cut corners with me on the price for the ranch. I expect I'll be sellin' to him, the deal bein' purty near as good as closed. But with Pearson waitin' to buy I can get more money out of the Easterner. Thet's the main reason I let him stay instead of kicking him off. Well, here comes a Mexican hand. He'll take care of your horses. Come on in."

But Cort shook his head. "I wouldn't risk it, Bat. A few weeks ago Pearson and some of his hooligans threw an ambush at me on the way back from Tucson, thinking I was loaded down with gold from Bruckmann's big safe. I just keep enough down south to pay for goods, the rest in Tucson. So they threw an ambush at me and we had quite a little scrap of it. I got one of his men and creased another before I drove them off and then made a run for it with one fast pack mule."

"He won't make any trouble in my house," was the grim reply. "And, anyhow, now that you're here to buy the ranch I'll go in and order thet outlaw to drift."

Cort finally acceded. He took a slicker roll from back of the pack animal's saddle. "What happened to them two unbranded hosses you took from the 'Paches after thet fight this mornin'?" Batton inquired.

"I stopped by Mrs. Larrabee's house and gave them to her," Cort said. "She's having a tough time since the Apaches got her husband two years ago. I urged her to give up that little place and get out of there to town. I told her there was no telling what would happen to a pretty woman like her, living here all alone. If some of these road agents or desperadoes happened to drift by some night. I feel sorry for her."

Batton eyed him in the dusk and grinned loftily. "The same way I felt sorry fer my wife, who was a widow, too.

86

Three weeks later she wasn't a widow any more. She was Mrs. Batton. Ain't no woman in the world can attract a man like a purty young widow. Men just can't resist 'em. So I reckon I'd better go over in the mornin' an' make her move over here, what with this raid on the stagecoach today. You shore came along at the right time, Jim, and only by the grace of God. If you hadn't, thet Anderson gal would start in bein' a 'Pache squaw tonight, or she'd have hed her throat cut in case Hardy and his men closed in. Comin' out from town Anderson told me all about thet runnin' fight an' about how he knowed you back East. Thet girl was all ears. Then Anderson sorta opened up to ask me a few things about you, but he didn't get far. Well, let's go inside to supper. I'll go to work till I find a buyer fer her little place and the few head of stock. Anderson might want to add it to his holdings, if he buys. If he doesn't, I'll sell to you, Jim; but only on condition you stick around here fer a day or two until we get the deal closed."

"All right," Cort agreed.

Force of habit made him slip the repeating rifle from its scabbard. He went with the rancher up across the flat, flagstoned veranda and into the big living room with the arch of the dining room just beyond. He felt ill at ease and uncomfortable at sight of Neely and her family, Hardy in immaculate blue, and Pearson. Six years in the desert alone had taught him to prefer solitude to a crowd. He stayed in Tucson only long enough to take care of business, because the call of the wastelands was always upon him. He ate in small, out of the way restaurants, avoided bars, and then headed back southward again to make lonely camp, cook his supper, and then lie there with his head propped up on the saddle, smoking and thinking.

Now his chaps made swishing sounds and his spur rowels clinked on the floor as, Winchester and slicker roll in hand, he flollowed Batton into the house.

"Ho, Ma, look who's here!" he boomed at his wife. "Come fix him up with a room an' let him wash up a bit. Hurry it up, Jim, or you'll hev to eat supper all by yourself."

Mrs. Batton had excused herself from the table. She came over and shook hands with Cort. Neely and the others sat staring. He had not, she noticed, even looked in her direction, and yet he knew she was there. He couldn't have helped knowing. And he was ignoring her.

"Hello, Jim, you Apache-shooting rider," Mrs. Batton greeted him. "You come along with me and I'll fix you up with a room. Pa, you go back an' eat with the folks. Go ahead and begin supper, folks. I'll eat with Jim."

Cort followed her down the hallway of the south wing and Batton went back to take his place at the table. If he noticed the strained look on Lon Pearson's face or the poker expression on Major Hardy's, the shrewd rancher said nothing. Many strange things had happened along the Santa Cruz. He only knew that Hardy had been a smiling, genial officer when he had come in with Neely after presenting her with the two bolts of contraband silk taken from Cort's five-pack mule train. He wasn't now. He was all military officer.

Neely broke the awkward silence. "I saw through the doorway that Jim had only one pack animal. He must have sold those other two horses he captured from the Apaches this morning."

It might not have been the right thing to say, in view of Hardy's presence and what had occurred there, but the day's events had filled her mind with one man and one man only; and by some strange combination of circumstances he was now on the ranch. She suddenly felt her appetite gone.

They were helping themselves to the steaming food now. Neely saw Batton fill his plate and then reach over

88

and pick up one of the little green pellets from the bowl and chew on it before taking the first bite of meat.

"No," the rancher said, chewing lustily. "He didn't sell 'em, Miss Anderson. He gave 'em away."

"But I thought he wanted them for himself," she exclaimed.

"Maybe he did. But it just happens thet over west of here on my boundary there's a woman named Kitty Larrabee. She's one of the purtiest little tykes you ever saw —not a day more'n twenty-three. Her an' her husband took up some land over by Greasewood Springs to git a start farmin' an' raisin' a little stock. They wuz married when they was kids. They wuz doin' all right, too, till he went out after the stock one evenin' an' she heard a rifle shot. A couple of renegade 'Paches had slipped up an' shot him off his hoss. But she's a dead game little woman if there ever was one, an' she stuck it right out by herself, tryin' to make a go of it alone. I tried to git her to come over here an' live with us, but she's got as much pride as good looks. Howsomever, she's havin' a hard time of it. So Cort took them two hosses of hisn he got from the raiders an' led em' by to give to her. He's allus helpin' out folks like thet, an' there's many a fambly twixt Tucson an' the *Blanco Oros* who'da gone hungry except for Cort."

He spooned more potatoes and reached for another of the green pellets, chewed it.

Neely sat there, and fires of jealousy shot through her. She didn't know why. But she told herself that when a man would go out of his way to help a pretty young widow of twenty-three, then there must be something more to it than charity.

"Anyhow," the rancher went on, "he's plumb worried about her since thet raid this mornin', what with renegades an' outlaws"—this for Pearson's benefit—"roamin' around the country. So tomorrer we're just goin' over there an'

89

make Kitty come here to live. She's got no business bein' over there alone."

"Of course not," Neely murmured.

"Jim put a purty good scare in her today," Batton went on, quite unaware that every word about the girl was a stinging barb in Neely's breast. "If you buy this layout of mine, Anderson, you oughta take over them springs from her. They're worth their weight in gold. It'll add one more big green bit of pasturage fer your cattle. Then, too, Miss Anderson here might find it a bit lonesome all alone on a ranch, after livin' in the big cities. Kitty would be a good companion. She can ride like a man, shoot a rifle if she has to, milk a cow, or do just about anything else. You oughta find something for her to do."

"I'm sure we can," Mrs. Anderson put in. "That's a splendid idea, Mr. Batton. By all means, bring her over here at once."

Pearson spoke up. "Sounds like a good idea all right," he said. "But just suppose that Mr. Anderson didn't buy the ranch?"

"Why not?" asked the Easterner.

"Because," the raider said, "that's why I'm here. I've had my eye on this place for quite some time. I'm prepared to bid against Mr. Anderson for the purchase of it."

In the silence that followed Batton's chuckle came softly. "Now thet's what I'd call one of them coincidences. You see, it jest happens that Jim dropped in on his way south from Tucson for the same reason. *He* wants to buy it too."

Neely unconsciously thought of the woman Kitty. Was that why Cort wanted to buy the ranch? Was that why he was responsible for the fact that the woman would be brought there tomorrow?

Hardy had taken little or no part in the conversation. But he seemed to read Neely's thoughts, and he was still remembering the humiliation that morning when he had

90

found himself facing a showdown with Cort and the Red-headed stage driver over the events that had taken place following the killing of the Apache raiders.

"I expect," he said, "that Jim is doing the same sensible thing so many more of these smugglers are doing: finding it the wise course to quit while their skins are whole. That last pack train the Army took from him probably convinced him—"

He didn't finish the rest of it, for Mrs. Batton and Cort came in beneath the arch leading to the big front room. Cort was washed and his dark hair was slicked down. He had removed his gun-belt.

He nodded a curt greeting to Pearson, said, "Hello, Bert," to Major Hardy, nodded to the others, and sat down beside Mrs. Batton.

Chapter Thirteen

MRS. BATTON said, "All right, Jim. You've had a long hard ride across the desert from Tucson with only camp cooking. I want you to fill up that plate and eat like a horse. You're too lanky. You need more home cooking."

"I hear," Lon Pearson said to Cort, "that you sent a bunch of Apaches to the Happy Hunting Ground today. You're a good man with a Winchester, no doubt about that."

"You ought to know," Cort said coldly over his plate. "The last time you and that outfit of yourn tried to bushwhack me I got Peg Leg with a lucky shot from a running horse and creased one of the others. That fellow Smith, I think. How bad was he hit?"

Batton half rose from the table. "Hold it, boys," he said. "This is my home until it's sold. All men who meet here will forget any quarrels."

"Fair enough, Batton," Pearson smiled. "No doubt about it—Cort and me's got a few things to settle, but we won't do it here. Right now I'm interested in two things: this wonderful food and buying this ranch from you."

"We'll talk about it in the morning," the rancher said, and his veiled glance at Anderson was filled with satisfaction. "Cort wants to buy the place too."

Cort had reached for one of the little buckshot-sized objects. He chewed on it and began eating.

"I'm going to try one of those," Neely exclaimed. "I've been sitting here filled with curiosity, watching you eat those, Mr. Batton, and now Jim is doing it. Pass me one, please."

Cort ate with his head down over his plate. He was uncomfortable and regretted he had come. He realized now that it wasn't coincidence Neely and her folks had been on the stage. Batton had met them at Vail and brought them to the ranch. The rancher was looking at the girl, and grinning with open amusement.

"I wouldn't do it, Miss Anderson," he advised. "I just wouldn't try it at all."

"But why not?"

"Well, it's like this," he exclaimed, his eyes twinkling. "The human body can build up resistance against almost anything: strong seegars, chawin' tobacco, whiskey, and so on. Now you don't look like a young woman who'd smoke seegars. If you tried it, you'd git sick as a dog the first time. But if you kept at it—an' a lot of women in America smoke 'em—you'd git to like 'em. Same way with chawin' tobacco or whiskey. The first chaw would

92

make you sick, the first drink would make you pie-eyed. But if you kept on at it, you'd soon git to like 'em both."

She was holding up one of the pellets in her hand, looking at him. "But what has that to do with these?" she protested.

Batton chuckled. "Them's the hottest peppers ever growed in the earth. They're hotter than them dried ones there, an' them *chilis encurtidos*—thet means pickled chilis —are plumb sweet beside what you got in your hand. Now down here in this country we eat a lot of Mexican food. The hotter it is, the better we like it. But you got to develop a taste fer it. You bite into thet, miss, an' you'll think you've just clamped down on the red-hot end of a branding iron."

She placed the pellet back in the bowl. Her father was obviously interested. He reached for one, holding it between his fingers and looking at it speculatively.

"Why, Mr. Batton, we have highly spiced foods in the East, too. This doesn't look that bad. I believe I'll try one."

"Ma," the rancher said to his wife, "git the pitcher of water handy."

Anderson bit down on the pellet and began to chew. His face changed, he opened his mouth, and then he was coughing violently, handkerchief out, gasping and reaching for his water glass. He drank in gulps, unmindful of the laughter. He got up and went to the window, making *whooshing* sounds in an effort to blow the heat from his burning mouth. It was on fire. He came back and got more water, tears were in his eyes now. Batton was grinning delightedly and reaching for another chili to go with his meat. He turned to Neely.

"All right," she laughed. "I believe you. Father has always boasted about how he liked hot foods. I'll bet he won't again."

Cort sat there eating, taking no part in the loud laughter, hoping only to get finished as soon as possible. By the

93

time he came to his dessert Anderson was coherent again, though his mouth was still burning. He looked at the rancher. Then he began to laugh too.

"Batton, I'll buy this ranch without further inspection. I like it here. I've never eaten food like this, never seen such a wonderful country or so delightful a home. I've worked hard to make a fortune. I almost broke my health in a drive for money. Now I see what I've missed. I'm going to relax and take life easy. I'm going to learn how to ride a cow horse and shoot a gun. But I know nothing about running a ranch. I'm as ignorant about the cattle business as a child. So I'm going to buy the ranch, and I want you to recommend a good man to run it for me."

"I'm open for the job," Pearson said, though his bold eyes were on Neely.

That brought silence. Major Hardy stirred his coffee and looked at Batton. The rancher's eyes were upon Cort.

He said, with studied casualness, "Thet's plumb generous of you, Pearson, but Cort has knowed this family a long time. Jim, why don't you dig in here an' run the outfit fer a while till Anderson learns the ropes?"

Cort looked at Batton. He saw Hardy's eyes upon him, and he saw the anger, the fear, the uneasiness in them. Cort didn't care a bit about Neely any more—that was all over——but this man hated him. He had kissed Neely there at the stage solely to let Cort know that she was now his girl.

"All right," Jim Cort said. "If it's agreeable with the new owner, I'll take over until he can find another man."

That was all. He finished, rose, and the others followed suit. They went through the big living room and out to the chairs on the long, flagstoned veranda. The moon was up, bright and clear, the night warm. From down among the cottonwoods two hundred yards away glowed the fires of the troopers. Their laughter came plainly. From the Mexicans' quarters over to the east guitar music floated from the open doorway of one of the adobe cabins.

Cort leaned against the wall, rolled a cigarette, lit it, and then strolled down the porch of the west wing. A huge cottonwood grew just beyond the end, throwing out shadows in the night. Cort moved on past it, walked a hundred yards to where a wagon showed in the moonlight. He went over and sat down on the tongue, smoking and inwardly cursing himself for taking the job. His decision had been inspired by resentment toward Hardy, a blow back at the officer for taking his pack train, gloating over him about Neely, telling her who and what he was. Jim Cort . . . desperado, smuggler, gun fighter.

He knew Hardy and the man's driving ambitions. He could still remember that time years ago at the Point when he had had to ask permission to speak to the man who now sat on the front porch, wearing the insignia of a major in the cavalry. Hardy had displayed his talent for leadership, and discipline, even then. He had proven it in a dozen forts, until he finally was assigned to Fort Huachuca; and here he had proven it again.

He'd got several Apache raiders, and at the same time he'd got Jim Cort's pack train. Cort was glad now that Sailor Morton had stolen it. Had Bert Hardy caught him with it and tried to take it, there would have been a shootout, with Cort the victor, and a fugitive from he U.S. military authorities.

He sat there on the wagon tongue in the moonlight, smoking one cigarette after another, his tactiturn face showing nothing of his thoughts. He heard the voices from the front porch, laughter, and then he saw her coming toward him in the moonlight, her white dress gossamer.

She had seen the glow of his cigarette.

"Jim?" she asked hesitatingly.

"Yes," he said.

95

She came up to him, to where he sat with his back against the wagon box, resting on the double trees.

"I wondered where you had gone. May I sit down?"

"It's your wagon now, Neely," Jim Cort said. "I only work here."

"I can sense the bitterness in your words, Jim, there is so much I want to say—about all those years when we were so much younger. And now, out of a clear sky, you are here; you and Bert and my family. I'm all confused."

"You'll get over it. It just takes time for adjustment. I had to get adjusted to the desert too."

"You have. I recognized you the moment I saw you from the stage," she said faintly. "I suppose shallow thanks are not in order after the service you rendered us today, saving our lives, but I wish to extend them to you, Jim."

"I didn't know you were on the stage," he said harshly. She saw his hard face in the glow of the cigarette butt as he pulled furiously on it; a brief outline in red that faded again. "I left Tucson yesterday afternoon and rode until dark, got away again at daybreak. I knew Red was coming out this morning, and I paralleled the road, keeping to the gullies and off the skyline. You learn that in the smuggling business. I just happened to be in the right place when the Apaches hit, that's all. I was thinking of Red and Ace, not the passengers."

"I'm glad you're here. I'll feel much safer now."

"I'll be here until I can get another man. Red. I'm sending word to him tomorrow. He's an ex-cowpuncher who knows this country, and that job of driving the stage is beginning to get on his nerves, what with holdups by Lon Pearson and his gang and raids like that one today. He wants to quit and go back to ranch work."

"Pearson?" she gasped out. "He held up the stage?"

"He was masked, but Red knew him. He—"

He didn't finish. Another figure was coming toward them in the moonlight. Major Hardy.

He loomed up. "Oh, there you are, Neely. I have some news for you. The deal for the ranch is completed, and your parents are giving both a housewarming and a farewell party for Mr. and Mrs. Batton. It will give you an opportunity to get acquainted with all the neighbors—and I assure you the fort will be fully represented."

"Why, that's grand, Bert. I think it's a wonderful idea. What do you think, Jim?"

He got up, tossing away his final cigarette. From over by the Mexicans' cabins came the twang of guitars and more singing.

> Noches de Mejico.
> Cuando los nubes esta en mundo,
> Yo voy con mi tristeza.

"What are they singing, Jim?" Neely asked. "It's a beautiful song."

"Night of Mexico," he said a little gruffly.

"Translate it," she ordered.

"Nights of Mexico. When the clouds are in the world, I go with my sadness, or sorrow. . . . I'd better go down and see about my horses. Good night."

He was gone toward the distant corrals, and the two looked after him. Hardy sat down beside her.

"Bert," she whispered, "he hates me. He treats me like I'm mud beneath his feet. He resents my presence."

He sat down beside her. "Does he?" he asked, and she caught the slight edge in his voice. "He hates you, and yet he took the job here. I envy him, being so close to you. Neely, I have two weeks' leave coming, a reward for capturing his pack train of silk and killing those Apache raiders. I want to spend it here on the ranch with you; and when it's over I want to go back to the fort, with you with me—as Mrs. Hardy."

97

Chapter Fourteen

CORT WENT down toward the corrals. They lay circular in the moonlight, with the various sheds and one big feed barn beyond. This was where Batton stored his alfalfa for the blooded horses. Nearly a dozen cows lay in the milk pen, chewing contentedly while their calves wandered around outside. It was quiet, and peaceful, and Cort saw the end of a dream. For months he had been planning to broach Batton on the subject of buying the ranch. Now it was too late, and an unkind fate had brought the new owners out of the past, including one whose face haunted him.

He was fighting against it, and there was little emotion on the surface. But the emotion of six years ago had come back with a rush; and again Jim Cort cursed himself for taking the job.

A sound came from behind. He turned from the corral fence. It was Lon Pearson.

"Nice night," Pearson said.

Cort said, "Yeah," and let it go at that.

The raider leaned against the fence, a square shoulder against a cottonwood post. He was rolling a cigarette, his features now sardonic in the darkness.

"So you're taking over as major-domo?" he asked.

"Looks that way."

Neither of them were packing guns. This Cort regretted. He hadn't forgotten that attempted ambush.

"Sailor Morton was plumb upset about you takin' his gold," Pearson said over the lighted match cupped to his lips.

"I was plumb upset over him taking my pack train," Cort answered. "So I sold it to him for forty-five thousand dollars. My Indian helper picked it up and hid it again. A fair swap."

"How'd you know he'd end up with me?" demanded the raider.

Cort sneered. "He's a man of the sea. When he ducked out with that pack train loaded with silk, he wouldn't hit across the desert. He didn't know his 'navigation,' as he called it. I knew he'd stick to the river and follow it. And I knew that he was bound to run into your camp in time. He'd blow in there, stiff from the long ride, tell you his story—at least the part about meeting me and knowing where my camp was located. He'd mention the gold he saw with me. You knew I was on my way to Tucson— he might have mentioned the emeralds I bought from him. And I knew you too well. With me in Tucson, you could risk back trailing to my camp to try finding my cache. So I simply wrote a note on the spot, when the fight broke out, gave it to Red Calf, my Indian helper, and had him first pick up the sailor's gold and then go on burning the breeze back to camp to my cache. So the sailor is riding with your raiders now, eh?"

"He's one of my men," grunted the raider. "And he's aimin' to get back that money that you stole from him."

Cort looked at him in the moonlight, and again the sneer crossed his hard face. "And you're aiming to help him?"

"I've got a score to settle with you. But I'll do it in my own time and in my own way. They made a mistake in hiring you to ramrod this outfit, Cort."

"I'm going to send word to Red, the stage driver, to come out right away and take over. I have no intention of staying. By the way, he recognized you when you held him up west and north of Bensen the last time. I'm just warning you, in case you get any ideas. Red's an ex-cowpuncher, and he's not afraid of the devil itself. You get too many ideas about this ranch—or Neely Anderson—and you might get them backfired into your face. Just a warning."

"I'll take care of that," growled the raider. "I got a few irons in the fire I ain't talkin' about."

"Leave them lay while you're a guest of this ranch. That means a truce between us while you're here. I'm still willing to call it quits, Pearson. You tried to take my pack outfit, thinking I had a load of Bruckmann's gold in it, and I protected it. If you came off second best, losing one man and another wounded, that's their hard luck. I'd call it even."

"I'm not callin' it even," Lon Pearson said, and dropped his cigarette butt. He ground it into the powdered dung by the corral with a boot heel. "So now that the ranch is sold, I reckon I'll pull out tonight."

"Good idea," Cort said. "And as of now I reckon your presence is no longer welcome on this ranch at any time in the future."

"The girl, huh?" jeered Pearson. "Afraid me an' the major will be too much competition, eh?"

He laughed and went on toward the house. Cort strolled over to a small adobe bunkhouse not far away and close by the Mexicans' cabins. There were three men in it. One of the others, LeRoy, was probably still riding hard tonight. The remaining one hadn't returned from Vail. Five men.

Cort introduced himself to the three as the new foreman and told of the sale of the ranch.

"So they swung the deal, eh?" one of them, a tall, mustachioed man of thirty or so, asked. "I been hearin'

100

the boss, an' Missus do a lot of talkin' about it after they got back from the trip to Tucson. And you're the new foreman, Cort?"

They knew him only by sight and casual meetings at the corrals when he had come to and fro on his trips. He had always stayed in the ranch house.

"Just temporarily, Hank. I want you to saddle up a good horse in the morning and go to Tucson with a message for Red, the stage driver. He made the run down into Tombstone today and will be back on the return trip tomorrow. He'll blow in about dark after a twelve or thirteen-hour run. Tell him that ideal ranch job he's been complaining about not finding is here at Batton's, working for the Andersons. Tell him I said to pack up his wife and kids and what furniture he wants to bring and come on down here right away."

"All right," Hank replied. "You said just temporary. Red taking over?"

"Yes, and he'll be a good man. They don't come any better. But maybe you'd better stroll over to the house and talk over the trip with Anderson, just to make sure. Got an extra bunk here? I'll be moving in with you boys."

"Shore. That one in the corner is empty. And yo're lucky. That Mexican woman who cooks fer us is the best ever. Lordy, the grub she don't shovel out for us."

Cort didn't say anything about the fight at the stage. They would find out in time. He and Hank went toward the house and Cort entered his room from the wing door. He was gathering up the belongings—his shaving outfit and spare clothes—and packing them back into the slicker roll when somebody knocked on the door. It was Major Hardy.

He stood there in the doorway, and there was an almost friendly expression on his face. "May I come in, Jim?" he asked politely. "I'd like to talk with you."

"Come on in," Cort said, and went back to his packing. "You can talk while I'm wrapping this slicker roll."

Hardy came in. "You're leaving?" he asked in obvious surprise.

"Just moving down to the bunkhouse with the boys—where I belong," Jim Cort grunted sourly. "Sit down, if you like. What's on your mind, Bert?"

"A truce, Jim. You put me in a bad spot today, in front of my men and also in front of the Andersons." He sat down on the bed and removed a cigar from his blouse.

"You put yourself in it," Cort said. "If you kissed Neely for my benefit, it was wasted. The past is dead, finished. You got the kiss, but you wasted the effect on me. It wasn't necessary."

"Hmm. I see. But you took the job just the same, and I think it was to spite me. Wasn't it?"

"Yes," Cort said. "You kind of made things bad for me, too. That pack train the big sailor had run off with was mine, all right, like you guessed." And he told of the man's entrance into his camp and the subsequent events leading up to its capture by Hardy. "But I'm glad he stole it. If you'd tried to run me down and take it, I'd have shot you out of the saddle, let you lay, and gone on. I mean it, Bert. Now I'm going down and stay with the boys until your friend the stage driver can get out here to take over and ramrod this outfit."

"And then?" softly puffing on the cigar.

"I'm drifting. New range. Buy a good ranch somewhere."

"What about this woman Kitty? She playing any part of it?"

"That's my own private business, Bert," Cort shot back at him.

"I like the idea. From what I hear of her, she'd make you an ideal wife. You're a frank man, Jim, so I'm going to be frank too. I was a bit afraid that Neely would let

102

that stagecoach business today, and the part you played in it, turn her head and make her forget her position and family name and what ah—"

"And what I am," sneered Cort, lashing savagely at the buckles. "If that's what you're worrying about, Bert, forget it. I'm not in love with her. Maybe she does disturb me when I look at her, but it's the same thing that disturbs any man who's been months away from a town when he sees a beautiful woman. I don't have to tell you—you're a desert man too."

"I know exactly what you mean, Jim, and I understand. That makes my purpose here much easier to explain. I want to call a truce with you. Forget what's happened between us in the past and be friends during the remainder of the time you will be here . . . that is, while we're both here. I have two weeks' leave due any time I wish it, my men are tired, and now that the redskins' last raiding party has been cleaned out of this part of the territory I'm going to stay here for a while and take in the housewarming for the Andersons and going away party for the Battons. Shall we shake on it?"

He got up and extended his hand. Cort shook.

He said, "All right, Bert."

He got ready to go, picking up his rifle and slicker roll. Hardy sat on the bed again, smoking thoughtfully. Something in his mien said there was something else on his mind. Finally he spoke.

"Jim, now that you'll be leaving soon, and now that we're friends again, I've something else to say. Again I'm going to be frank. Jim, the Army is my career. It's a passion with me."

"Heck, you don't have to tell me. I haven't forgotten my first year at the Point, when you were finishing up. You made it tough on us every opportunity you got . . . and I'll bet a hundred dollars that if I went down and talked to your men they'd say you still do."

"They would be correct. I believe in human discipline in all walks of life. The masses haven't either the intelligence or the initiative to rule themselves, so there must be leaders. That is particularly true in the Army. We must have discipline. But while we're being so frank, I'll continue. I want promotion more than anything else in the world—promotion and Neely as my wife. I'm working hard to get both. I suppose you already know—or have guessed—that you have been partly responsible for my recent promotion to the permanent rank of major. The Old Man at the fort asked me to get results—just one smuggler pack train, if nothing else. I set out to way-lay you, to wait until you came along. The Indians were just a lucky break that comes to a man once in a lifetime. I brought in your pack train and a report of successful engagement with a band of renegade Apaches. The Old Man kept his promise. He went to the general and got me these oak leaves I'm wearing."

"All right, I'm not complaining," Cort grunted. "I got forty-five thousand dollars in gold for them, plus nearly thirty thousand profit from a certain man who bought the emeralds paid for with the gold. I bought them from the man you pursued with the pack train. He had stolen the train from me during the fight, I got back the gold. I'm satisfied."

Hardy's cigar had gone out. He lit it again, smoking thoughtfully.

"That makes me feel better, Jim, now that we're friends once more as we were in the old days," he said. "But, Jim, that isn't enough for me. The Old Man at the fort is retiring next year. He's a full colonel.. They might send out a man to replace him and they might pick his successor from one of the officers."

"You, for instance?" Cort grinned thinly.

"If things break just right. We're after Geronimo, but we can't find him. If I could bring him in, when the general

104

and the whole cavalry have failed, I'll have a pair of eagles on my shoulders and command Fort Huachuca within one year. You know where he is."

"Yes, I know where he is," Cort admitted. "I talked for an hour with him not too long ago."

"I see," Hardy answered thoughtfully, and pulled harder on the cigar stub. "And you could lead me to him. Jim, I saved my inheritance when you spent yours. I'm pretty wealthy; I've the kind of wealth and position a woman of Neely's position must have. You owe it to her to help me."

"I don't owe her anything except six years of heat and loneliness in the desert," Cort said harshly. "Not that I'm kicking. It was the best thing she could have done for me. I came out of it a certain type of man—maybe not your kind, but I'm satisfied. Maybe she did me a favor."

"Good. That's better yet. She did you a favor," Hardy said eagerly. "So I'll speak plainly, Jim. Take me and my men to Geronimo—no matter where he is, even across the Mexican line—and there's twenty-five thousand dollars in gold waiting for you."

Cort already had rifle and slicker roll in his hands. He had been waiting for Hardy to finish. Now he leaned over and blew out the lamp. His voice came through the darkness.

"That's the military men's job, Bert. You said so yourself today."

"You're refusing?"

"No. I'm just telling you to go to blazes."

Chapter Fifteen

HE WENT out and Major Hardy sat there in the darkness for a few moments, suffering the bitterest disappointment of his life. A colonel's eagles almost within his grasp in a year or so, increased prestige as the fastest rising young officer in the West—Neely to add prestige and share his—and it was gone, blown out as the light had been blown out by Cort, because that hard, bitter man had refused Hardy's offer of gold.

Hardy got up and went out, closing the door behind him. He stared down the hallway, and saw Lon Pearson standing in the doorway of his own room. The raider grinned as the officer started on by, after a curt nod.

"Come in," invited Pearson, grinning again. "You look all upset."

"Thank you, but I haven't time," Hardy said stiffly.

"I've had an ear cocked at this door for the past five minutes. You and Cort forgot to close yourn. So come down off that military high horse, Major, and come in. Maybe you can get them eagles yet."

Something about the man's voice caused Hardy to accept. He went in, and this time the occupant of the room closed the door. Hardy saw with surprise that the outlaw, too, was packing. Pearson caught the look.

"Yep, I'm pullin' out tonight," he said. "No reason for me to stay around, now that the Andersons have bought the ranch. Anyhow, I got business of my own to attend to. Sit down, Major, I'm goin' to talk."

Hardy sat down. He looked at the raider. "Well?" he demanded crisply.

Pearson sat down opposite him, in a big chair. "You just sit back an' listen while I talk. I reckon you know by now that Cort an' me ain't friends, even if we didn't go at each other's throats tonight. I got a score to settle with him. It's private an' we don' have to talk about it."

"It won't be necessary," Hardy said coldly. "I heard the conversation at the table this evening. You tried to ambush him and one of your men got killed and another wounded. So, sir, whatever you have to say, I'm willing to listen for a moment before joining the others on the veranda."

"You'll listen longer than that," chuckled the raider. "I got plenty to say, and you'll like it, I think. I ain't fooled a bit by that new friendship business between you and Cort. You both hate each other—you in particular because he turned down your offer to lead you to Geronimo."

Hardy was interested despite the contempt he held for the outlaw. "Do *you* know where he is?" he asked bluntly.

"I wish I did," grinned Lon Pearson. "I'd take that twenty-five thousand in gold of yourn in a hurry. No, this is something else. Like you and Cort, I'll speak plain. I heard this gal of yourn talkin' to Miz Batton in the kitchen a little while ago when I come by. They was by themselves except for a couple of Mexican women washin' dishes, an' who couldn't understand English. This gal you want to marry is all busted up because of Cort. She's in love with him and you know it! You won't come out and say it, but deep down inside of you *you know it!* You're on pins and needles, just hoping that he'll pull out in a few days like he says he will and leave you a clear trail. But she's a beautiful woman and I'll bet you a hundred dollars that all that feeling he had for her in the old days—I heard her tell Miz Batton all about it—has come back. And, Mister, you ain't

107

got a chance, if it has. You ain't got a chance. Not unless you and me do something about it. Well?" he demanded.

"I'm listening," snapped Hardy. "Get to the point."

"You want a promotion and you want this gal Neely. And I'll bet a thousand this time that you can't get her as long as he's around. Not unless something is done about it. I can do something about it. I can have Cort arrested right here on this ranch and put in irons by a United States marshal; or better yet, let you do the job. Ha! You look kinda interested now, Major. Here's how it works. Back in the desert are sixty alien Chinese. They was brought from China on a ship called the *Sally Ann,* the same ship Sailor Morton was first mate on. They was unloaded off the coast of Mexico onto a schooner owned by a Mexican merchant and smuggler named Velasquez, who delivers Cort jewels and stuff—includin' that silk you took. Velasquez sent 'em up the Gulf of California to the mouth of the *Rio de la Concepcion.* From there they was put in flat-boats and taken to Cort's camp up the river. They're mine, of course, not his. He won't smuggle Chinese. But I knew he was on his way to Tucson to sell about sixty thousand dollars worth of emeralds, along with that silk you grabbed; so I went south to his camp and took delivery on them Chinese. We're workin' 'em across the desert slow, at night, on foot. I was going to have a marshal step in and grab them, and frame Cort for it. But just supposin' that about the time this house party got under way them Chinese showed up here on this ranch? You could round 'em up with your soldiers, put Cort in irons as the man who smuggled them in, and then back-track to his camp to prove it. You just got one of his pack trains. Sposin' that about the time this house party got going, you got sixty of 'his' Chinese and arrested him. You get more credit as an efficient officer, the gal Neely changes her mind about him in a hurry and turns to you, and Cort goes to a Federal penitentiary for about fifteen or twenty years. How does it sound?"

108

Hardy was a man of decision. He made one now. He looked at the raider. "How much?" he asked.

"Five thousand, bargain price, since I'm squaring up with Cort," was the reply.

"It's a deal," Hardy said. "And if you breathe a word of this, Pearson, I'll never stop until the cavalry has hunted you down like we're hunting these Indians."

"Fair enough," agreed the raider.

They began working out the details.

The long ride by stage and hack, the excitement, the sudden turn of events by which she had found both Cort and Hardy on the ranch—they produced a soundness of sleep that lasted until after eight the next morning. She rose, dressed, and went out into the big ranch house. The place appeared deserted until she went into the big kitchen and saw her mother talking with Mrs. Batton while several Mexican women peeled potatoes, cut meat, and otherwise made preparations for the noon meal.

"I'm hungry," she announced.

"Well!" exclaimed her mother. "You ought to be. Sleeping in like this."

"Where is everybody so early?"

Mrs. Batton let go with a peal of laughter. "Lord almighty, girl, it's late. Everybody has been up and around here for hours. You're on a ranch now. Pa and your father have gone after Kitty. Your pa's going to make her an offer on the place. Major Hardy is down with his men. One of the boys left at daylight to go to Tucson after Red to come out here and take Jim's place."

"Where is Jim?" Neely asked quickly.

"He rode out at sunup with the boys to get the lay of the ranch. He knows it pretty well, but there's a few things he wants to find out so's he can pass them along to Red when he gets here with his wife. We've got a big 'dobie cabin all ready for them. Now you set down here and have

109

a cup of coffee and I'll have one of the girls fix you some breakfast."

"I expect," Neely smiled, "that I'd better start getting up with the rest of you. But I was tired. I never slept so hard in my life."

She finished breakfast and went out to look the place over, wandering down by the barns. Lon Pearson was nowhere around, and for this she was glad. She didn't like the way the raider's bold eyes played over her.

She looked out across the field to where the Mexicans worked, and listened to the chug of the big steam engine pumping water into the tanks and for the irrigation of the alfalfa. Presently she returned to the house and then went down across the wide expanse in front of it to where the cottonwoods lay below. She saw Hardy, and she saw troopers busy soaping saddles and cleaning their guns. Their eating equipment lay spread out on blankets in the sun, scrubbed and shiny. Hardy saw her coming and came to meet her, his hat off.

"You look lovely," he greeted her.

"Thank you, Bert. But I'm restless. I feel mean, sleeping in this way while everybody else was already up and gone. What are you doing?"

"Getting the troopers ready for a bit of inspection of equipment."

"Why?" she wanted to know.

He smiled patronizingly at that. "It's like this, darling. An idle trooper is a grumbling trooper. But if he's kept busy under strict discipline, he has no time for grumbling. So I keep them busy putting equipment in tiptop shape."

"But I thought they were here to rest?" she asked.

"They're resting. Sergeant Toland!"

"Yes, sir."

Toland came up, throwing a sharp salute. "Sergeant, inspection of equipment and mounts at ten sharp. Extra

110

duty for any trooper whose equipment is not up to standard."

"Yes, sir."

Toland saluted and Hardy walked with her back toward the big house. He was spending every minute possible with her, she knew. They went into the big living room and she played the piano and sang until time for him to go back to his men. At eleven o'clock she heard the sounds of rattling harness in the lane and looked out. The big hack was coming up at a trot, and she saw a girl sitting in the back seat. Neely stood there as the rig came to a halt and Batton helped Kitty Larrabee down. Hardy was coming up from below. He paused and Batton grinned.

"Major, this is Kitty Larrabee, who's coming to live here for a while. Anderson just bought her out, lock, stock and barrel—and a good bargain he got. I'll have to send one of the boys over to batch on her place and look after things. Kitty, Major Hardy."

"Now I know this place is a paradise," Major Hardy laughed gallantly. "Two pretty women in one place at the same time. I'm glad you and Neely are not both at the fort. You'd wreck discipline."

Neely had come down. She saw lovely brown hair, brown eyes, and a face just freckled enough to make it attractive. But there was more than that: a certain character that showed courage, determination, and latent sorrow. In that moment Neely Anderson's heart went out to the girl, as they were introduced.

They all went toward the house and Kitty took the room vacated by Jim Cort. Neely went in with her to help arrange her things. They were already good friends by now and were chatting happily.

"This was Cort's room until he moved down with the men last night," Neely said. "He's Father's new foreman."

"Yes, Bat told me," Kitty replied. She used the word

111

"Bat" in speaking of the rancher as naturally as though speaking of someone her own age. "Where is Jim?"

"Out on the ranch somewhere. They've sent for Red, the stage driver who brought us from Tucson to Vail, to come out and take over. Jim's leaving."

"Leaving?" gasped out Kitty a little too quickly, and Neely felt all tight inside. "When?"

"As soon as Red takes over. You've known him a long time, haven't you?"

"Yes, Neely. He rode by a couple of days after my husband was killed. Bat and Mrs. Batton had come over with some of their men to help bury him. Jim stayed on the place for a few days while I went to Tucson. I had to get away. I couldn't stand it. I thought I didn't want to come back, but we had started that place as mere kids; and, anyhow, there wasn't anything else to do. I haven't any parents."

"What you need to do is get married again."

Kitty smiled at that; in fact, she almost laughed. "I had plenty of offers. Cowboys, prospectors, and one bank robber who offered to go straight. He was shot and I nursed him back to health. And the soldiers too. There was a handsome lieutenant from the fort who always came to me at every opportunity but they shipped him to another post."

The two went out again. Neely didn't want to talk with Hardy. She felt a strange restlessness. They went down past the bunkhouse toward the corrals, and it was about then that Cort and another rider came up. Neely saw him look at the girl as he rode over. He swung down with a single lithe step and removed his hat. Neely had never thought his sun-bronzed face could light up with anything like the friendliness that crossed it as he came over.

"Kitty, I'm glad. I can sleep better now, knowing you're here."

"I wanted to thank you for two horses, Jim," Kitty

112

smiled. "I sold the place to Mr. Anderson this morning—everything. But those two horses. I'll keep them to ride."

The dinner gong had rung. Neely said, "Jim, won't you come over and eat with us?"

"Thanks," he said, and again it was the flat, emotionless man speaking. "I reckon I'll eat with the boys."

Chapter Sixteen

DURING THE next few days the Circle B took on an air of festivity; there was a tense and growing excitement. Word had been sent out to surrounding ranches: Haines and the Double Arroyo outfits and several smaller neighbors would be there in full force. Ace's folks had come back from Tombstone and would come over. There was a fat young yearling in the milk pen, eating its head off at a trough filled with grain, alfalfa, and milk mush, while the Mexicans dug a barbecue pit and laughed while they worked. Anderson had found an old pair of leather chaps somewhere and was riding around the ranch on a gentle pony, as proud as a school boy. Hardy kept his men busy on night guard and on patrols that were unnecessary while he spent all possible time with Neely and Kitty, who by now were fast friends. Sergeant Toland had begun to make excuses to come up to the house, and to talk with Kitty.

"I think the man's in love," Hardy laughed to Neely. "Not that I blame him, darling. Love is a wonderful thing. If he and Kitty got married, perhaps I could recommend him for a commission as a second lieutenant. We could even make it a double wedding."

Neely didn't answer that. She and Kitty rode together almost every day, partly because Neely loved it and partly because she hoped to run into Cort. She seldom saw him. He was out, seemingly, from dawn until dark, and he never came about the house any more. He stuck strictly with the men, eating in their cook shack.

And then Red showed up one day. He drove a wagon, his wife in the seat beside him, a Winchester across his knees. In the back of the wagon, piled high with household belongings, were three impish-looking boys of seven, nine and eleven respectively. They were all redheaded.

He rolled into the yard in front of the house and his "whoa, blast you!" to the team might have been a yell at his stagecoach four. He got down and Batton came out to grip his hand.

"Hello, Bat," the ex-stage driver greeted him warmly. "What's this job I'm supposed to do? So this is yore layout? Allus wanted to see it. Where's Jim?"

The three *muchachos* had jumped down and were looking the place over as Red's buxom wife descended. The Andersons came out, and Red shook hands all around.

"Howdy, Miss," he greeted Neely. "I see you didn't turn grey-headed from the purty little fracas we had on the way to Vail."

"Little," gasped out Neely, laughing. "I was never so scared in my life."

"Neither was I," Red admitted seriously. "I knowed what was comin' up. They shot Ace off the seat first. They coulda got me as well, an' they coulda got any of the hosses from ambush when they got Ace. But them red devils like their sport. They wanted to git rid of Ace first, then chase us a bit till they could down one of the wheelers or a lead hoss. Then they'da knocked me off the seat with a shot an' gone to work on the passengers. Thet big devil

114

comin' up at a run on the off side was gettin' ready to shoot one of the wheelers, knowing my six-shooter was empty an' I couldn't handle a Winchester with one hand. That was when Jim busted in. Lordy, I never was so glad to see a man in my life. The minute he came poundin' outa the greasewood with that repeater in his hands I knowed things was goin' to be all right—even if the cavalry was late. Howdy, Major."

Hardy's face was all poker as he stuck out his hand. Red's words had bitten deep. His wife was looking around.

Mrs. Batton said, "I'll have one of the Mexicans drive your stuff out to the new house. You folks come on in and have some coffee."

"Sounds good," Red agreed. "I could use some. I got my old saddle in the back end of that wagon. It'll feel good to get a hoss under me—Hey!" he bellowed in a bull-lunged roar. "You, Wyatt, git down off the top of that house! Poke, you and Willie come down outa that tree before I git a switch and bust all three of you."

They went inside and drank coffee, and then Red left to help unload the rest of the furniture. The house was a comfortable four-room adobe: two bedrooms, a combination living and dining room, and a kitchen with a big cook stove. Batton had built it with the idea of having a married foreman, but had discovered that when a man builds a ranch from the ground up he can't turn things over to a foreman. Batton had supervised everything himself, and the new house had lain vacant.

Cort rode in at sundown with Hank and the rider LeRoy, who had returned by now. Ace was buried in Tombstone's boothill, one man who hadn't been killed there in a saloon gunfight. Cort was tired, dusty, and hungry. He swung down and saw Red, and a grin split his face. It was the first time that Neely, over by the milk pens where the Mexicans were busy with pails, ever had seen him really smile. The two men shook hands.

115

"So you got here, Red?" Neely heard him say. "I'm glad. I'll show you the ropes before I drift."

"Why the blazes should you?" Red demanded belligerently. "No reason to, Jim. Why don't you stay on here as foreman? I told Anderson that maybe I'm gettin' too old to straddle a hoss any more. I've allus been interested in this irrigation business. Heck, Jim, I could handle the fields and you could take care of the cattle. How come you got to go?"

They spoke in low voices then, and Neely strained her ears to hear the words. She heard the name of "Red Calf" and the name of Lon Pearson.

"The devil you say!" Red ejaculated. "Like that, eh? What do you suppose is back of it?"

"I don't know," Neely heard Cort answer, "But it's trouble, Red. I don't like the looks of it."

"Neither do I. You reckon that stage robbin'——" And Red finished with an unprintable word followed by others Neely couldn't hear because they were spoken in a lower tone of voice.

"All right, Jim," Red finally said. "I'll keep my eyes open and my six-shooter handy. Like you, I don't like the looks of things."

Neely turned away from the corral, Kitty beside her. The other woman had heard too.

"What do you make of it, Kitty?" Neely asked.

"I don't know," Kitty replied. "But I'm like Red——I don't like the looks of it."

"Would it do any good for you to ask Jim? I know it would be a waste of time for me. He hates me, Kitty. He won't even look at me. But you——he——"

"It might; I won't know until I try," the other answered. "You wait here and I'll go over and see him."

Neely saw her go over, saw the friendly greeting Cort gave the lovely Kitty, and again a pang shot through her. Cort was avoiding her as though she had the plague. And

116

it had begun to inspire resentment in her. She had almost thrown herself at him, tried in every way possible to tell him of her regret about what had happened in the past, her gratitude that he had saved the lives of her parents and herself. He had ignored her. That was why she was more genial and smiling toward Major Hardy.

Kitty came back. She shook her head. "He wouldn't say anything, Neely," she said. "He's never treated me like this before. He's always been so kind and considerate. Now he's almost curt."

"He couldn't be kind to anybody," Neely flashed, her temper getting the best of her.

"That's where you're wrong. He's the finest man I ever met. For two years, after Bob was killed, he always stopped by going and coming from Tucson. He brought me things from town. He helped out in a dozen ways. Last spring, when a gang of horse thieves came through here, raiding the country, he sent some Indians up here to watch the place. Five of them. I never was so scared in my life as the morning I went out to the corral and saw those five Apaches sitting their horses right by the milk pen. I thought my heart would stop. Then one of them grinned and spoke to me and said something to the other four, making them stay behind. This one, Red Calf, came forward on his pony with a slip of paper in his hand. It was a note from Cort. The other four were his brothers. They were to watch the house and stock until the gang of thieves went through. They did, too. I got a funny feeling, going about the place and knowing that Apaches were watching me . . . every move I made. But I didn't lose my stock, and one day they simply disappeared. I told Cort just now I heard the name of Red Calf. He just scowled at me and said I'd better come back to you. I don't understand it Neely."

"Well, I do," Neely answered angrily. She was Irish and she was a little proud of her temper. That temper was getting away from her. "All right, then, I'll hate him too. I'm glad he's leaving."

"No, you're not, Neely. But—look, here comes the major. I wish there was another like him around. I envy you."

Hardy came up and led the two of them away, playing the part of the gallant officer with one on each arm. He was in fine spirits. He had even relaxed a bit and allowed his men more levity, more leisure time around the house. Sergeant Toland had come up to the house for supper on two occasions; and Hardy made sure that the big, middle-aged sergeant was seated next to Kitty.

Preparations for the celebration went on. And back in the desert, twenty miles away, Lon Pearson lounged with his men and watched over the Chinese.

They were a pitiful, frightened group now, all under guard. Four of them—the four who had spoken English brokenly—were dead. The bearded outlaw Smith, whom Cort had wounded, had shot them. The haul in gold had been good. The aliens were even richer than Pearson had dreamed. Sailor Morton lounged about, taking his turn at guarding them, a borrowed Winchester over one arm. He swore oaths every time Cort's name was mentioned.

"You real shore," Smitty asked that day, as Pearson was saddling up, "this deal will go through like you planned?"

"Yep," grunted the raider, tightening his cinch. "It's all set. I'm goin' in now to see if Hardy got that five thousand like he promised. I'm meetin' him tonight at ten back of the corrals. If he delivers like he promised, then we'll keep our part of the bargain. I think he will. That means that 'party' they're havin' is going to have about *sixty* uninvited guests. Then we get the drop on Cort and put him in irons."

"And this sojer plays the big boy with the girl, hey?"

"Maybe," grinned the raider. "But if something happened to him, then I might have a clear field, eh? Just a

118

thought, Smitty, just a thought. You watch the Chinese and follow orders. I'm heading north."

He mounted and dropped out of the hidden arroyo and presently struck the course of the river. The afternoon sun was midway toward the horizon, but he had plenty of time. He rested his horse in the shade of a cottonwood, smoked for an hour, watered the animal, and resumed his journey. The sun went down and darkness came on. The moon was a little late now, but it was up by the time the raider pulled up a half mile from the Circle B Ranch buildings and looked at his watch. A quarter of an hour left. Just time to make it. He went on at a walk, keeping to the deep shadows of the "Alamos," and finally saw the outlines of the corrals with the lights of the ranch house and various other quarters beyond. Pearson approached the corrals at a walk, hand on his gun. Then he saw the shadow move and pulled up sharply.

"Hold it!" he called out sharply. "Don't move."

"Major Hardy." came the reply.

Hardy came out from where his body had been blended with the trunk of a giant cottonwood. He carried a heavy canvas sack in one hand.

"Got the money?" Pearson asked, low-voiced.

"I gave you my word," came back the curt reply. "Where are the aliens?"

"Under guard about twenty miles from here. Twenty miles to be exact. They'll be all over this ranch by day after tomorrow night when the party is in full blast. Gimme the money, Major."

"When you deliver the Chinese, Pearson. Don't try to pull a gun on me, and take this. Sergeant Toland has you covered with a rifle. I merely brought it as evidence of good faith."

Pearson laughed. "All right, Major. But you're too cautious. You forget I got a personal stake in this game

119

with Cort. I wouldn't double-cross you. See you day after tomorrow night."

He turned and walked his horse away, disappeared into the moonlit night in the shadows of the cottonwood. From somewhere nearby came the click of a rifle hammer being let down and Sergeant Toland came out of the shadows. He came up and grounded the butt of the single shot 45-70.

"All right, Sergeant," Hardy said crisply. "Put this money back in the hiding place. And I think that within a few months you'll get that commission I want you to have."

"Yes sir," Toland replied.

He took the heavy canvas bag. He was under orders, and he didn't like it at all. It was a heck of a way to get a commission.

He hadn't wanted one in the first place.

But when a man served under Major Hardy, he obeyed orders . . . and he kept his mouth shut.

Chapter Seventeen

ON SATURDAY morning Cort shot the fat yearling through the head with a rifle, and the Mexican ranch butcher, standing by with a sharp knife, cut its throat. Cort and Red hooked on to it with their lariats and dragged it out of the corral and onto a big tarp spread out in the sun. Two other Mexicans went to work with knives and began skinning it. They gutted it and rolled out the entrails, saving certain of them for a delicacy known as son of a b—, but

120

called "son of a gun" for the sake of politeness. The entrails, with parts of the liver and heart, would be ground up and mixed with flour and certain other ingredients and cooked in a big cast-iron pot. Over by the barbecue pit the red beans had been cooking since early morning. They would be cooked under a slow cottonwood fire for nearly fourteen hours before being allowed to simmer and cool.

By noon the cut up parts of the yearling already were turning on the spits over the fires, along with the carcass of a goat. The Mexicans liked their goat meat.

In the area just back of the kitchen, covering one hundred yards to the corrals, post holes had been dug and a line of tall posts set up forty feet apart in a huge circle. A wire had been strung between the posts. On this wire would hang the lanterns for illumination. Directly in the center the Mexicans had built a dance platform on two-by-fours, sixty feet across, with a small platform for the musicians. The big piano had been moved out of the living room and now reposed beneath quilts to protect it from the hot sun.

Nobody was working that day, except the soldiers. They were not idle, but they were grumbling.

"Dawg-gonnit, Sergeant Toland, I'm plumb sore," one of the troopers growled to Toland that Saturday. "Here I been lookin' forward all week to doin' a hot fandango with some of them pretty Mexican gals, and what happens? We cain't go. We got to stand *guard* over the visitors in case *Apaches* show up! If you don't mind, I think I'll go down by the river where nobody can hear me and cuss the major for a while, right out loud. I've been wantin' to tell him off for a long time."

"I know how you feel," grunted the sergeant, just as uncomfortable as the disgruntled trooper. "But in the Army you obey orders and you don't ask any questions. The major says you'll stand guard with loaded rifles—and by glory, you'll stand guard."

The afternoon wore on. The meat was browning on the

spits now, the beans and "son of a gun" bubbling in the big cast-iron kettles. A big table had been built near the barbecue pits. On this would be stacked meat, bowls of sour pickles, pickled chilis, peach cobbler, and the huge pans of cornbread the Mexican women were busily cooking.

From hidden trunks in the Mexicans' cabins had come gaily colored cloth, and every dark-skinned infant that could toddle had been decked out; the girls in gay dresses and ribbons, the boys in "charro" costumes. From all over the place came the chatter of Spanish, laughter, and talk from the big house. The "old" Don and the "new" Don were certainly doing things up in style. The gay mood was broken only once, when Red's three *muchachos* got into a fight with a group of little Mexican boys and the ex-stage driver had to run, bellowing, to separate them.

Cort stood in the doorway of the bunkhouse and laughed harder than he had laughed in years as Red beswitched his three offspring in front of a group of grinning Mexican children.

By three o'clock that afternoon the first of the visitors began to arrive. Neely went out to greet Haines and his wife, their daughter and her husband. Two riders came with them, for they were a small outfit. John Sellers, owner of the Double Arroyo, put in an appearance shortly afterward with their unmarried son and four DA punchers. In no time at all the Circle B seemed to be overrun with people of all sizes and ages, many of them Mexicans.

Neely tried to be every place at once, greeting visitors and welcoming them to the ranch. She heard talk of drouth, prices for cattle, Apaches, the silver being taken from Tombstone by the ton. She met a woman named Malden, and discovered that the visitor was Ace's mother.

"I'm glad to be here, Miss Anderson," the plain-faced woman said. "I understand you were on the stage when the Indians killed Ace."

"Yes, I was, Mrs. Malden," Neely answered, not quite knowing what to say next.

"He was a good boy. He saved his money and sent part of it to us to help keep the place going. There wasn't a better boy ever lived."

"I'm sure of it, Mrs. Malden. If you'll come inside, I'll show you where to put the children tonight when they get sleepy. It looks like all the rooms will be filled, but nobody will need them. The older Mexican women will watch over them while we dance. They say it will last until daylight."

"It will." Ace's mother smiled. "You don't know these western people—but you'll get to know them in time."

Afterward Neely found Kitty and they wandered down toward the corrals. The corrals were filled with saddle horses and teams, while all around the house were buggies, wagons, and even two ox carts. Over by the bunkhouse a dozen men were grouped around, and several more were down on their knees close by the wall. They were shooting dice; and from the sounds coming from within, Neely knew that a poker game was in progress.

She saw Cort. He was leaning against the wall of the bunkhouse, taking no part in the proceedings, his face as blank as ever.

"Hello, Jim," Kitty greeted him warmly. "Just look at that crowd out there. We're going to have a time tonight."

"I imagine," he said.

"And don't you forget to dance with Neely and me. Understand?"

"I haven't been on a dance floor in six years, Kitty," he answered, smiling. "I wouldn't know how any more."

"We'll teach you, won't we, Neely?"

"If Jim wants to dance with me . . . like he used to in the old days." Neely smiled.

"Maybe one or two." Cort smiled back at her. He did want to dance with her. He wanted to hold her in his arms just as he had when they were so much younger. But his

123

gear was all packed. He was pulling out in the morning. Red had told his wife and she had told the girls. They knew.

Major Hardy came strolling up. "Hello, Jim," he said affably. "Looks like quite a celebration coming up tonight. I've just had a courier. A message from the Old Man himself. He heard about the celebration and will be here at any moment."

Hardy didn't say that he himself had sent one of his men to the fort with a note to the colonel. For Hardy was playing it shrewdly. He wanted the Old Man himself present tonight when the soldiers rounded up those Chinese and Hardy put Cort in irons.

"Glad to hear it, Bert," Cort said casually. "It should be a nice fandango. Your men don't often get an opportunity to dance with so many pretty girls. They undoubtedly will enjoy it."

"As a matter of fact," Major Hardy announced casually, "they won't be taking part in it. They'll be on guard."

Neely had turned to him in surprise. Nearby a man on his knees had just let out a whoop as he raked in his winnings from a lucky throw of the dice.

"But why, Bert?" she asked.

He smiled at her patronizingly. "Neely, it is the job of the soldiers to protect the civilians out here. Just because the last bunch of raiders off the reservation has been accounted for, it doesn't mean that there aren't more, or some of the Sonora Apaches up from across the line. These lights strung on wires can be seen for miles. I can't risk it. I'd like to see my men relax and enjoy themselves, but duty comes first. They must stand guard."

"You standing guard with them?" Cort grinned sardonically.

"They will be in charge of Sergeant Toland," Hardy said stiffly. "I have certain social obligations, as the officer in command."

124

He turned and left and Kitty laughed. Neely said, "Jim, I thought you and Bert were friends now. He told me so. What you said wasn't very kind."

"When are you leaving?" Kitty asked, though she and Neely already knew.

"In the morning," he said.

"Where to?"

"Tombstone first. After that . . ." He finished it with a shrug.

As for Hardy, he went back to his men to give certain last instructions to Sergeant Toland. The troopers would be allowed to go up and eat of the barbecue as soon as it was ready and then return for their weapons. A few of them would be stationed in plain sight. The others would be down by the corrals and in among the cottonwoods to catch and arrest the Chinese. Pearson's riders would flee at once—and the soldiers had strict orders not to fire upon them.

Hardy started back toward the ranch house, and then he saw the eight men in blue clattering into the yard. Sight of them made his heart leap. The Old Man had arrived with several junior officers.

Colonel Eblen swung down and shook hands with the host as troopers came running to take the horses. There was hand-shaking and saluting all around.

"Well, Colonel, this is a surprise," Batton greeted the officer. "Glad to have you with us, sir. Of course, you'll stay all night, though you won't get much sleep. Don't know where we'll quarter your men, though. The rooms are all filled up with kids. Anyhow, these young officers won't be interested in sleeping tonight. Not with all these purty gals here. Come along with me and I'll get Ma and we'll see about a place for you."

The officers with the Old Man went down to where horses already had been taken. The colonel followed Batton inside, bowed to Mrs. Batton, and presently found himself in a big, comfortably furnished room in the east wing, with his orderly.

"Send Major Hardy to me at once," he ordered.

Chapter Eighteen

PRESENTLY HARDY came in. He saluted the colonel.

"I'm glad you arrived, sir," the major said.

"Sit down, Major. I want to talk with you. Now tell me what this is all about?"

Hardy sat down. This was one time he was at ease and not stiffly formal. He felt the weight of his new rank on his shoulders, and tonight would be the high point of his life to date.

"Very well, sir," he said. "You wanted results and I've been trying to get them for you. Now I'm getting more. You already have received my dispatch concerning the stagecoach holdup by the remnants of the Apaches we wiped out when I brought in Cort's smuggler pack train. We were hot on their trail—a matter of minutes—when they attacked the coach. But this man Cort had accidentally happened there ahead of us and broke up the attack. My fiancée, Miss Anderson, whose parents have just bought this ranch, was on the coach with her parents. They were on the way here. I accompanied them for protection and to give my men a rest. While here I found out that Cort was bringing in sixty Chinese to deliver to Tucson.

126

By the way, he's posing as the foreman of this ranch until his aliens arrive."

"When are they due?" the colonel asked sharply.

"Sometime tonight, sir. He plans to slip them by the ranch, along the river, while the celebration is in progress."

"How did you find out all this, Major?" demanded the older man.

"My men have been out on daily patrols since we arrived here, sir," Hardy answered smoothly. "They discovered the men, came back and reported. I gave orders not to molest them, merely to keep them under observation. Then I happened to overhear Cort talking, and found out the aliens are due tonight. They are in the custody of a gang of desperadoes headed by a man named Lon Pearson. You've heard of him?"

"Of course," grunted the colonel.

"He and Cort are supposedly enemies but are actually pardners," went on Hardy smoothly, thinking of that five thousand dollars he wasn't going to pay. Had Cort accepted his proposition to lead Hardy to Geronimo, the new major hadn't had any intention of paying that twenty-five thousand dollars either; not when he could bring in the body of the man he so hated. Pearson had been right: There would be no chance for Hardy with Neely until Cort was either disgraced or dead. "They'll both be here tonight. At the right moment I'm going to clap them both in irons. I wanted you to be here when it happens, sir. These ranchers are complaining that the Army isn't on the job. I wish to give them a convincing demonstration that we are."

"Very well, Major. I leave the matter in your hands. It is to be presumed that your plans are well laid."

"Yes, sir."

"Good. Now I'm hungry. I'm going to clean up and find out about something to eat."

"The barbecue is ready by now, sir. It's almost sundown and the dancing will begin at dark.

"They'll dance until daylight. I'll wait for you outside and make the introductions."

He left, and the orderly came in and went to work shining the colonel's boots. Hardy went outside. The lanterns, strung on the high wire, were lit and people were laughing and talking in little groups as they ate barbecued beef, beans, son of a gun, peach cobbler, and drank big cups of steaming black coffee. Screaming children seemed to be running around everywhere, playing tag, and Hardy saw his men eating hungrily before returning to their camp down among the cottonwoods to get their weapons. He saw the blue of the junior officers and spoke to a lieutenant here and there. The night was warm and he was content.

He strolled off down by the corrals, half hoping to see Neely. What he saw was a big blond man on a horse come up and swing down. Lon Pearson. The raider saw him and let the reins dangle. He came over, grinning. Hardy's eyes went cold.

"What are you doing here?" he rapped out. "You ought to know better than to put in an appearance at a time like this."

"You ain't talkin' to one of your soldiers now, mister," grinned Pearson. "You give *them* the orders. You dam' well better not waste any breath giving *me* any, because I don't take 'em from any man. I'm here because I wouldn't miss this shindig for all the Chinese in China. I see they got a liquor keg set up over there for the visitors. That's for me. It'll sharpen my appetite for supper. I'm hungry."

"Where are your Chinese aliens?" snapped back the officer.

"I left 'em comin' this way this afternoon. Smitty's pushin' them hard to get here about nine o'clock when the festivities are in full swing. We'll shove 'em up right against the corrals and then my men will light out. The rest is in

128

your hands. You just be sure none of them soldiers of yourn get over-anxious with their trigger fingers and plug some of my men. They could shoot the sailor, if they wanted to. He's pretty upset because he hasn't got a chance to make Cort cough up that forty-five thousand in gold Cort's Apache Indian stole. I told the fool he might as well forget it, but he's still grumbling. Well, I'm going over for a drink."

Hardy frowned and watched him go. He had told the colonel that he was going to arrest Pearson. Actually he had no such intention. Pearson the prisoner would talk and bring a military investigation. Toland had orders to shoot the raider for resisting arrest, if Hardy failed to do so. The officer salved his conscience by thinking that he was doing the people of the territory a favor—which was the truth. The man was a raider, robber, horse thief, smuggler, and probably a murderer. The territory would be better off without him, and Hardy wanted the credit.

Those three passions—for promotion, Neely, and wealth —still dominated his life more than ever, and he would let nothing stand in the way.

He went to find the colonel. As he walked toward the big sprawling adobe ranch house he saw Jim Cort. Cort was striding toward the barbecue table where Lon Pearson was helping himself. Both men wore pistols.

Cort came up and looked at the raider. "I told you to keep off this ranch from now on," he said in a low voice. "You're not welcome here."

"I know it," grinned back Pearson. "But I ain't worried. You're too plumb good mannered to make a ruckus here in front of all these people, an' you know it, Cort. I knowed it too. Batton wouldn't like to see his last shindig on the ranch busted up by a gun fight that you'd lose. So I come on in, and you ain't going to do a thing about it. Batton won't like it either, but he won't say anything."

129

"I know he won't. He knows like I do—that nobody but an ornery bushwhacking road agent and horse thief would have the crust to do it."

"Sure I got gall—I'm made of it," chuckled the raider, spooning up more beans from the cast-iron wash pot. "And you can call me all the names you want and I won't do anything about it—tonight. After tonight, when we meet, you'd better come shooting. I'm squaring up for my men."

Down by the house, the colonel had just emerged. Hardy nodded with a jerk of his head. "There they are, sir. The wiry-looking man on the left is Jim Cort—the former James Van Cortland—whose pack train of silk I captured. The other is Pearson the raider, who's bringing in the Chinese tonight. They're probably discussing plans for the night and how to get the aliens by here without being seen. Cort is already packed to leave in the morning, supposedly heading for Tombstone. What he actually plans to do is catch up with Pearson's men who are herding the Chinese."

"What is their destination?" the colonel asked.

"Tucson, sir. There's a Dutchman who owns a store there who deals with the smugglers. He buys their silks and jewels and 'dobie dollars, and anything else the smugglers like Cort bring in. I presume he'll take these Chinese and send them out in little groups to Los Angeles, San Francisco, and Seattle, to the friends they have waiting."

"I see. Very well, Major. I'm here merely as a guest. I presume that the matter can be left in your hands."

"It can, sir. There will be no slip-up. My men are on guard in a circle around the ranch. They have been alerted. We'll take over the Chinese and then I'll put Cort and Pearson in irons."

"Very well. Here comes Mr. Batton."

Batton came up with Anderson and grinned.

"Well, I see you're all slicked up for the dance, Colonel," the rancher observed. "But you look hungry. Come on over and try some of that son of a gun. Ain't nobody in the world can make it like my Mexican butcher."

"Son of a gun?" asked the colonel. "I seem to remember vaguely hearing of it. What's it made of?"

"Calf guts," said the rancher, and then went off into booming laughter at the look on the colonel's face.

They went toward the tables to get plates and scoop up food from the big kettles. Cort was striding back toward the bunk house, and Neely saw him go. She had witnessed his conversation with Pearson.

She walked past the circle of lighted lanterns and followed him. She wanted to talk with him. He deliberately avoided her, and now he was leaving in the morning. And she didn't want him to go. That flash of temper long since had gone. She knew only that she loved him, that he was leaving, and that nothing in the world seemed to be able to sway the hard-faced, implacable man who had been James Van Cortland.

He was going down by the corrals and she walked after him. Laughter came from the bunk house where the poker game had been in progress for hours, and would continue until daybreak. Horses and mules dozed in the corrals, some still harnessed. She saw Cort go by the end of the corral and disappear and she came up by a corner of it— and a scream that never came welled up in her throat as she saw the Apache Indian.

He stood some forty yards away in the shadows of a big cottonwood tree. He was in full war paint, with a terrible-looking ochre streak of paint laterally across his cheeks and nose below the fierce eyes. She wanted to cry out, to warn Cort, but fear left her frozen.

Then the Indian stepped into view with a rifle in his hands. She saw Cort turn at the sound of a *hoo-hoo* and

131

walk towards him. They spoke rapidly in Spanish and she heard harsh, guttural answers.

Then the Indian was gone like a fleeting shadow.

Neely turned and almost fled back toward the platform where the musicians were beginning to tune up.

Chapter Nineteen

THE BIG PIANO had been uncovered and now reposed beside the raised platform where three Mexicans with guitars and a rancher with a fiddle were tuning up. One of the women visitors was setting herself on the stool. They finished tuning and then Red walked out in the center of the dance floor.

"Git pardners for a square!" he bellowed. "There's room for two, so we'll make it a double square!"

Cowpunchers and ranchers scrambled to find women partners. The floor filled almost at once with two groups of eight each. Four men faced four women partners at one end of the floor and four other men faced their partners at the other end. Red stood in the center. Around the platform nearly one hundred men and women and children stood ringed.

The music struck up.

"Circle four in the middle of the floor," Red roared out, and the mill started.

Red stood there bawling out instructions to the dancers.

"Do-si-do. A little more dough, a little more dough," he chanted.

132

"Take yore pardner, pat her on the head,
"If she don't like biscuits, feed 'er cornbread."

Followed by,

"Hawg eatin' feed in a pen six palings high,
"If I'se that hawg, I'd git out or die.
"Whoop-souie!"

The dancers swung, do-si-doed, bowed, and continued the fast pace. The music didn't stop. You didn't stop music in a square dance until the dancers grew tired. Ten minutes later a man swinging his partner let out a shrill whistle. It was taken up in a chorus by the others and the music came to a halt. They had had enough. Sweating, panting men and women cleared the dance floor, mopping their faces with bandanas. The music struck up again, a waltz this time. Neely saw Major Hardy coming toward her to claim the first dance, and she spied Cort at the edge of the crowd. He was smoking a cigarette, his face expressionless. He wore a gunbelt, the heavy pistol low at his right thigh. She had somehow hoped that he would be the first to ask her to dance. She saw Kitty in the arms of a handsome young second lieutenant as she let Major Hardy's arms enfold her as they floated across the floor in time to the music.

Over his shoulder she saw Cort again, and she remembered his conversation with that wild Apache in full war paint. She stifled an inner shudder, her woman's intuition telling her that something was in the wind. She could sense it.

Hardy looked down at her lovely face, smiling. "This is the kind of thing I've dreamed about, Neely," he said. "You in my arms again. We give dances at the fort once a month. You'll have plenty to occupy your time there. I want you to come over and visit us right away and inspect the place. You'll like it there, Neely."

133

"I'm sure it's a nice place," she said, and they danced on.

The dance rolled on. A stream of people made regular trips to the big table to eat, and others—all men—went to the whiskey keg to drink from tin cups. The bold, swaggering Lon Pearson claimed Kitty for a dance, and she couldn't refuse him. Pearson had put his gun away somewhere. You didn't dance with a gun on at the ranch house celebration. It was a violation of custom and good manners. She was the center of attraction for all the young officers, who were fighting to get her as a partner. Neely saw and she was glad. Kitty needed love. She needed one of these clean-cut young officers to follow wherever he was sent. She was glad . . . until she saw Cort, gunbelt gone, striding across the floor toward where she and Kitty stood.

A young officer had just asked her for a dance, but Neely appeared not to hear and continued talking with Kitty; stalling until Cort got there. She would tell the lieutenant that she already had this dance.

Cort came toward them, his hat off, his blond hair slicked down and gleaming in the light of the lanterns hanging from the wires overhead. The harshness in his face had momentarily been replaced by a smile of pleasure.

"Kitty," he said, "it's been six years, but if you want to give it a whirl I'll try not to step on your toes."

"The way you say that, Jim, it sounds like you're saying good-bye," Kitty said.

"It is," he said. "I'm leaving in the morning, you know. I've got a few things to take care of."

Neely let the young officer claim her, sharp disappointment shooting through her. It was increased when, a few minutes later, she saw Cort at the edge of the crowd again. His gunbelt was strapped around his waist once more. She went to him, breaking away from the officers, and came up to where he stood smoking a cigarette. Red was assembling dancers for another double square.

134

"Jim," she said, "don't you think you're doing me a bit of injustice?"

"How?"

"Ignoring me in front of all these people who have now accepted me as one of them. Look at Father over there—chatting away with those ranchers about feed and cattle and water holes as though he'd been out here all his life. Look at Mother—coming from the house with ranch women who've been in to see about their babies. And you haven't even had the courtesy to ask me to dance with you."

He didn't tell her of the fear within him—the knowledge that he was in love with her as of old. He didn't tell her that he was remembering the past, that he was afraid he might weaken . . . and lose out to Major Hardy.

He masked his feelings by harshness.

"You seemed to be doing pretty good with Bert," he said. "He's had you for every other dance. In between, the young officers from the fort have been fighting over you. Why should I interrupt?"

"I went down to the corrals at dark to see you, after you finished talking with Lon Pearson. I knew you had just told him he wasn't welcome. I wanted to ask you not to have any trouble here tonight for our sakes—to let him stay. Then I saw that terrible Apache Indian. Jim, what does it mean?"

He shrugged his shoulders and dropped the cigarette butt to the ground, grinding it with his boot heel. "That was Red Calf, my Apache helper. He was here on business. Kitty knows him. So you can forget it."

"But he was in full war paint," she whispered.

"Yes," he said stonily, "he was in full war paint."

"Jim, what is it?" she asked. "What did it mean? There's trouble coming and I know it. Look at Pearson. He's wearing his gunbelt again and he's uneasy. And Bert—he's acting strangely."

135

"He's not acting strangely now. Here he comes to claim you for the next dance," Cort said.

Hardy came through and hooked a possessive arm through Neely's. He was all smiles. "Jim, if you're not going to dance with her, you haven't the right to keep the prettiest girl in Arizona out here talking with you. Come along, darling. This is our dance."

As she danced the number with him, she watched the crowd: Pearson with his gunbelt on, his eyes flicking to Cort; Hardy watching both men. There was violence and tragedy in the air and she knew it. There was going to be trouble before the night was over. Cort had warned Pearson that his presence wasn't welcome, and yet the man was there. There was that horribly painted Apache Indian who had spoken Spanish to Cort under the cottonwoods back of the corral. And she had seen Hardy glance at his big watch a number of times.

They finished the dance and Hardy went over to the colonel. He had his watch in his hand.

"It's almost time, sir," he said. "Another half-hour."

"Where are your men?"

"Stationed around the ranch in a circle, ready to close in. The aliens should put in an appearance almost any time now. Then I'll shackle Cort. I'd better get my revolver, sir."

"Very well, Major. You know your business."

"My plans are well made, sir. After tonight the worst smuggler and the worst outlaw gang of desperadoes in Arizona will be cleaned out. And the Army will have sixty captured alien Chinese on its reports in Washington. I truly regret that the general isn't here tonight. He would appreciate the work we're doing."

The half-hour passed, and then an hour. The colonel was fidgeting, casting glances at Hardy. Nothing had happened so far. Hardy was not dancing now.

Then, shortly before eleven, it happened. Red was in the

136

middle of a square dance, calling instructions, when the music suddenly stopped with a crash.

Hoof beats sounded, and a hundred pairs of eyes turned as a sweat-drenched horse loped past the corrals and into the circle of light.

It carried two riders. One of them, a black-bearded man of about forty, sat back of the cantle, holding another in the saddle. The other man was Sailor Morton. The front of his big chest was covered with blood and he was swaying. A woman screamed as the black-bearded, gun-packing man slid to the ground. He caught Morton as the sailor toppled from the saddle, easing him to the ground on his back.

"What's going on here?" Batton roared, pushing through. "Git back, folks! Git back!"

Morton was wheezing and gasping and working a big hand over his bloody chest. The squat, black-bearded man straightened as Lon Pearson came through the crowd.

"Lon, we're wiped out!" he cried hoarsely. "Apaches! They hit us a little while ago and got every man. Morton an' me got away into the desert. We had a tough time gittin' here. He's dyin'."

"Not yet," gasped out the sailor. "I'll live to slit a few throats yet."

"Apaches!" snapped out Hardy. "Where?"

"They're back a ways. I—"

And then women and children screamed and men cried out hoarsely as five savage-looking figures stepped into the circle of light behind Jim Cort.

"Look out, Jim,—look out!" Neely screamed. "Behind you, Indians!"

"Sergeant Toland!" bellowed Hardy. "Toland!"

"Hold it, Bert," rapped out Cort. "Your men are in custody, bound and gagged but not hurt."

Pearson had slipped into the circle and stood beside the

137

black-bearded Smith. They were looking at Cort, hands close to their gun butts.

"So you brought these murdering red devils in here—to this ranch," Hardy said to Cort. "You're under military arrest. I've got a pair of shackles waiting for you, Cort."

"Yes, I brought them here for two reasons," Cort said, and turned to one of the murderous-looking Indians who stood with rifles in their hands. They were Red Calf and his four brothers.

Cort spoke rapid Spanish and the Indian turned. A sharp, shrill cry broke from him. It was answered from all around as a dark mass of men—Chinese—appeared down by the corrals. Then from all sides, seemingly out of the very night itself, rose nearly one hundred Apaches in full war paint, ringing the frightened women and children and sending cold chills down the spines of the helpless men.

They closed in, ominous, silent, big single-shot 45-70's in their hands.

"Jim, what's the meaning of this?" Batton roared. "Why do you—"

"Hold it, Bat," Cort said quietly. He turned to the colonel, his face stony. "I believe you have an explanation coming, sir."

"I believe the Army does," replied Colonel Eblen.

"Don't believe him, sir," Hardy broke in, and Neely saw fear in his face. "There's the evidence I told you of. Sixty Chinese he smuggled in."

Cort looked down at Sailor Morton and a brittle grin came to his hard face. "Morton, you doublecrossed me and I made you pay for it. Tell the colonel who smuggled in these aliens."

"It was Pearson," got out the big man with the yellow beard, still on his back on the ground. "Only him and Major Hardy were going to frame Cort and put him in irons tonight. Hardy paid Pearson five thousand for the job."

"It's not true, sir," Hardy shot back. "That man—" He was pointing at Cort with leveled finger, and the finger was trembling. Back of Cort, the stolid-looking Apaches with the streaks of ochre paint across their cheeks and hooked noses waited, fingering their rifles.

Cort smiled, ignoring him, and said to the colonel, "A short time ago I quit the smuggling business, sir. On my final trip that man on the ground found out there were sixty Chinese merchants and other men of considerable wealth aboard a schooner in the gulf. He should have known about them—he was first mate on the ship that brought them from China and later up the coast to the Gulf. He stole a pack train of mine loaded with silk and tried to get away during a fight between Apaches off the reservation and a group of Hardy's men. Hardy there captured the train—not forgetting to hold out a couple of bolts of the silk for a certain lady. Morton joined Pearson's gang of desperadoes, and they went back to my hidden camp down in Sonora and brought in these Chinese. They were too stupid to realize that my Indian helper, Red Calf"— and he pointed to one of the Indians back of him—"was watching their every move. Red Calf burned the breeze north and told me about it. So I sent him back to Sonora after about a hundred men of his tribe to keep the Chinese and their guards under observation but not to attack. They followed my instructions."

He paused, his cold eyes on Pearson and the black-bearded Smith. On the ground Sailor Morton was grinning like a gargoyle, despite his wound.

"And?" prompted the colonel in a curiously quiet tone of voice.

"They followed my instructions, sir. They stood by and watched while that black-bearded man there by Pearson shot four of the Chinese who could speak a little English

139

and robbed the others—a crime for which I was to be blamed by Hardy. Hardy had come to me and offered me twenty-five thousand dollars if I'd lead him to Geronimo and help capture him. He said that you're retiring next year and that if he could bring in Geronimo he'd get your job and command of Fort Huachuca. He—"

"It's not so, sir!" cried out the major.

"You're a liar, Bert," Cort said calmly. "I overheard you and Pearson planning the frame-up in his room here in the house, when you thought I'd gone to the bunk house. You agreed to pay him five thousand dollars to push those Chinese into the middle of this celebration tonight, so you could clap me in irons in front of all these people and the colonel." He turned to the colonel, though Neely, standing frozen, saw his hand laying close to the big pistol at his hip. The Apaches had closed in now in a solidly packed ring. They couldn't understand what was going on, but Red Calf had told them what was in the wind; and this strange man *Jeem Corte* was their friend. He had refused white man's gold to betray their leader, Geronimo.

"So Red Calf reported to me every night," Cort went on relentlessly, "and tonight, following my instructions, these Apaches descended on the camp where the Chinese were now prisoners and wiped them out. But Morton and that man who brought him in seem to have got away."

Neely stood there, her hand on her father's arm, Kitty beside her. She saw in the glow of the lanterns the ring of vicious-looking Apaches, the silent, frightened women and children, and Cort facing Pearson and his *segundo*. She saw his harsh face, heard the relentless words that were destroying the career of an overly ambitious Army major.

"I see," she heard the colonel answer softly, "I'm beginning to see a lot of things now. But that still doesn't explain why these Indians are here in what could turn into a massacre if they got out of control."

140

Cort said tonelessly, "They want Lon Pearson, that outlaw leader who, among other things, held up the Tombstone-to-Tucson stage a short time back."

"You're a liar," snarled Pearson. "I never—"

"Yo're another!" roared Red from the edge of the crowd. "I was drivin' thet stage an' I recognized you, you dirty—" And Red spat out an unprintable word. "That mask didn't fool me. I'd know you anywhere."

"What do they want me for?" gasped out Pearson.

Cort ignored him, still talking to the colonel. "Last year Pearson and some of his raiders were down across the line in Mexico, trying to find my camp and get my gold cache. They ran into a small band of Apache women and children going to a new camp. Pearson took one of the girls for himself—and then cut her throat with a knife when she fought him. These Apaches never forget things like that, sir. So they've come for him. That's one of the reasons they're here tonight."

"Damn you, Cort—" Pearson screamed.

And then Neely saw him and the black-bearded man crouch, hands flashing to their hips. The night was split by gun flashes and the roars of six-shooters. She saw flame spurts lashing out from Cort's hip, saw him stagger back, and then keep on firing. The black-bearded man was down, coughing out his life, and Pearson had dropped to one knee, fumbling for his fallen gun. He half rose to his feet and then pitched forward to lie face down.

Slowly Cort sheathed the still smoking six-shooter. He had an odd look on his face as he turned to the colonel.

"The other reason they're here—these Apaches, sir— is because one of them is a representative of Geronimo, who is hiding in Mexico. He wants to come in and talk. Red Calf!"

The Apache stepped forward and Cort spoke to him in Spanish, an odd tone in his voice. Red Calf turned and spoke gutturally in Apache, and a man stepped into the

141

circle of firelight. He was fully six feet two inches in height, and the cowhide head-dress, adorned with two curved horns, proclaimed him some kind of warrior chief. He spoke gutturally to the colonel, Red Calf translated in Spanish, and Cort said in English, "Geronimo wants to have a talk with the general, sir. These men will return to Sonora tonight with any message you have."

The world was clouding up and he felt his legs beginning to get weak. He had to get out of there, something in his brain kept telling him. He had to . . .

He turned, stumbled and Neely's scream cut the night as he fell into the arms of Red Calf.

"He's shot! He's shot!" she was crying out, and he felt her arms around him as darkness blotted out the lights of the lanterns strung high on wires between the poles.

He came out of it, out of weird crazy dreams in which he was falling over cliffs and into bottomless pits, where Apache devils shrieked and yelled gleefully as they grabbed hold of him and began to stick knives into his chest. He fought and moaned and a woman's voice said, "Lie still, Jim. Quit struggling, darling. It's Neely."

Fire was still shooting through his chest as he opened his eyes. He was flat on his back in bed, in the room he had previously occupied. Neely sat on the sheet beside him and he heard her crying.

He saw other faces in the room as the clouds cleared. Red and the Andersons and the colonel and a young lieutenant who had medical instruments in his hands. An Army doctor.

He ceased his struggles and looked up. Neely had her arms around him. "Lie still, Jim. The doctor removed the bullet. You'll be all right. And I'm glad you got shot," she added fiercely.

"Why?" he whispered.

"Because now you can't leave," she whispered. "So I'm glad, glad!"

"The Apaches?"

"They're gone . . . back to Sonora with a message for Geronimo. The general will talk with him and listen to his complaints."

Red bent over and grinned. "Thet was some gun fight, boy. I wanted to give you a hand and square up with Pearson for robbin' my passengers, but like a dam' fool I couldn't get to my gun in time. It was on the piano under a quilt. Pearson and his *segundo* are done for, his gang wiped out, and you git the credit for it. Sailor Morton is dead. He kicked the bucket sometime during the excitement."

"Where's Bert?" Cort asked weakly of Neely.

"Hardy," guffawed Red, "is leavin' for the fort in the mawnin'. I heard the colonel talkin' to him. He had the choice of a court-martial or demotion. He took the demotion. He's now Second Lieutenant Hardy, subject to the general's final decision. What I want to know is why the blazes they didn't bust him back to mule-tendin' private, like I told him when you busted up thet raid on the coach."

"What I want to know," Cort whispered weakly, "is why the blazes you don't get out of here so I can use this good arm?"

"We're practically gone," grinned Red. "Come on, folks. I hear 'em bellerin' for me to come call another square dance. We'll bust up the place until daylight. Now thet you've got thet bullet—it was a .44, Jim—removed, you'll be up and around in no time."

They went out and Cort looked up at Neely, still bent over him. "I can still use this one good arm, Neely," he whispered.

"You won't have to use it, Jim," she whispered fiercely, and bent down to kiss him.

143

EXCITING WESTERNS
From Macfadden-Bartell

LAW OF THE GUN *by Paul Evan Lehman*	50-508	50¢
VIOLENT MAVERICK *by Walt Coburn*	60-460	60¢
ACTION AT THE BITTERROOT *by Paul Evan Lehman*	50-506	50¢
DRIFT FENCE *by Walt Coburn*	60-458	60¢
THE BUCKAROO *by Burt Arthur*	50-504	50¢
WAR ON ALKALI CREEK *by Lee Floren*	50-502	50¢
THE STRANGER FROM TEXAS *by Allen K. Echols*	60-457	60¢
THE COLD TRAIL *by Paul Evan Lehman*	50-500	50¢
BORDER JUMPER *by Walt Coburn*	60-454	60¢
LOBO VALLEY *by Lee Floren*	50-498	50¢
SQUARE SHOOTER *by Walt Coburn*	60-453	60¢
TROUBLE AT SUDDEN CREEK *by Al Cody*	60-451	60¢
WHEN TEXANS RIDE *by J. E. Grinstead*	50-496	50¢
SILVER GULCH *by William Hopson*	60-449	60¢
SHANNAHAN'S FEUD *by Al Cody*	50-494	50¢
GUNSMOKE BONANZA *by Chuck Martin*	60-446	60¢

All books available at your local newsdealer. If he cannot supply you, order direct from Macfadden-Bartell Corporation, 205 East 42nd Street, New York, New York 10017. Enclose price listed for each book, plus 10¢ extra per book to cover cost of wrapping and mailing.